S0-AHS-254

"Do you believe in second chances?"

"I don't know."

He reached for her hands. "Let's find out. Let's start over. Let's be like phoenixes and rise from the ashes."

"You mean that? You really want to try again?"

He released one hand so he could cover his heart. "Yes. You're a beautiful and successful woman. I'm even more intrigued by you now than I was fifteen years ago. I would so much like another chance to get to know you."

A light breeze wafted under the overhang and onto the gazebo. The air was ripe with spring. But it was Justin's words that made her catch her breath. "Oh." Her heart fluttered.

Justin moved closer. "We're adults now, Chandy. We have a past, and a sad one at that. But that doesn't mean we can't have a shot at the present. We won't know until we try."

She smiled up at the man she'd never really stopped loving. "Then, Justin McCall, yes. You've got yourself a date."

Dear Reader,

Welcome to Justin and Chandy's story. Love has the power to transform. For Chandy McDaniel, that's exactly what she needs. It's been fifteen years since a terrible tragedy left her overcome with grief and guilt she's never been able to shake. When her first love, Justin McCall, reenters her life, Chandy's torn between keeping her secret and sharing her pain with the man who caused her heartbreak.

Yet neither can deny the attraction humming between them, or the fact that the love they thought they had lost forever might just be hiding deep inside both of them.

This book is special. When I was writing it, every piece fell into place. The words seemed to flow from my fingertips and things occurred that surprised even me. So please enjoy the story as much as I did when I created it, and don't hesitate to contact me and let me know what you think. You can reach me through my Web site at www.micheledunaway.com or through my Facebook fan page.

All the best,

Michele

The Doctor's Little Miracle

MICHELE DUNAWAY

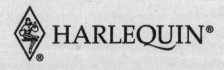

HARLEQUIN®

TORONTO • NEW YORK • LONDON
AMSTERDAM • PARIS • SYDNEY • HAMBURG
STOCKHOLM • ATHENS • TOKYO • MILAN • MADRID
PRAGUE • WARSAW • BUDAPEST • AUCKLAND

Recycling programs
for this product may
not exist in your area.

ISBN-13: 978-0-373-75327-7

THE DOCTOR'S LITTLE MIRACLE

ABOUT THE AUTHOR

In first grade, Michele Dunaway knew she wanted to be a teacher when she grew up, and by second grade, she knew she wanted to be an author. By third grade, she was determined to be both, and before her high school class reunion, she'd succeeded. In addition to writing romance, Michele is a nationally recognized, award-winning English and journalism educator who also advises the yearbook, newspaper, and student Web site at her school. Born and raised in a west county suburb of St. Louis, Missouri, Michele has traveled extensively, with the cities and places she's visited often becoming settings for her stories. Described as a woman who does too much but who doesn't ever want to stop, Michele gardens five acres in her spare time and shares her home with two tween daughters and eight cats that rule the roost.

Books by Michele Dunaway

HARLEQUIN AMERICAN ROMANCE
988—THE PLAYBOY'S PROTÉGÉE
1008—ABOUT LAST NIGHT...
1044—UNWRAPPING MR. WRIGHT
1056—EMERGENCY ENGAGEMENT
1100—LEGALLY TENDER
1116—CAPTURING THE COP
1127—THE MARRIAGE CAMPAIGN*
1144—THE WEDDING SECRET*
1158—NINE MONTHS' NOTICE*
1191—THE CHRISTMAS DATE
1207—THE MARRIAGE RECIPE
1251—TWINS FOR THE TEACHER
1265—BACHELOR CEO
1293—BABY IN THE BOARDROOM

*American Beauties

For all those at Show-Me Auto Body in Pacific, MO, who have patched up my cars over the years— and especially for Michelle and Dave for their kind words of encouragement. This one's for you.

Prologue

For Chandy McDaniel, life as she knew it was officially over. She wrapped her arms around her waist and tried to fend off the winter chill that had enveloped Chenille, Iowa, and her heart. She stood on the icy sidewalk, the wet slush from last night's snowstorm soaking through her tennis shoes. She didn't care. Nothing mattered when her seventeen-year-old heart was breaking.

"It's going to be okay. I'll write. Phone. Hey, don't cry." Justin McCall, her boyfriend ever since eighth grade, crooked his finger and lifted her chin. "You know I love you. Nothing's going to change even though I'll be in Chicago. I'll come back this summer. That's only five months from now. You'll see. Everything will be fine. We'll be together like we planned. This is just a detour."

Chandy blinked back tears. "It's our senior year. Couldn't you have stayed? Finished high school in Chenille?"

"You know I wanted to. But my mom said no. She needs me. She can't raise Derek by herself. We wouldn't be going to Chicago if my uncle wasn't there. He's promised to help out."

Justin's father had died suddenly of a heart attack, and the small life-insurance policy wasn't enough to make ends meet. Despite community support, the situation was dire. Mrs. McCall had been struggling with twelve-year-old Derek's behavior, and she had no family nearby to help. The closest was her brother in Chicago.

Chandy knew she was being selfish in wanting Justin to stay. But ever since the tall, shaggy-haired jock sitting in front of her in first-hour history class had turned around and pierced her with those baby-blue eyes, he'd been the only guy for her.

He wrapped his arms around her and then drew back. "Hey, I have something for you. Don't open until Christmas." The holiday was four days away. He reached into his coat pocket and withdrew a small wrapped box. He closed her bare, cold fingers around the present. "Promise me you won't peek."

She nodded and fought back tears. "I promise."

"Good." Justin's lips smiled but his eyes were sad. Behind them the front door slammed as his mom and younger brother exited the house. Justin's uncle had already driven away with the U-Haul truck containing all the McCall family's worldly possessions. As his mom and brother cleared the porch and headed to the car, the house was a silent and empty testament to the death of a dream. Icicles hung from the for-sale sign.

Mrs. McCall loaded Derek into the back of the aged SUV and called to her older son. "Justin. We have to go. It's a long drive. I'm sorry, sweetie. He'll write." She gave Chandy a sympathetic smile and, with a shiver, climbed into the driver's seat and started the engine.

Chandy and Justin had said their goodbyes last night, parked on the old Quarry Road. There, wrapped in each other's arms in the back of Chandy's car, they'd let the engine idle and the heat blow as they'd made love for the very first time. They'd always planned on waiting until they were married, but neither had ever expected this separation. They'd had it all laid out. Graduation. College. Marriage. Jobs at McDaniel Manufacturing. A house. Dog. Kids.

She failed to contain the tears, and they streamed down her face and froze to her cheeks. "I love you."

"Ditto." Justin used the words Patrick Swayze had said in *Ghost,* the movie out a few years back that they'd claimed was their movie. He kissed her gently and then stepped away as his mother honked the horn twice. Chandy held his hand, and he stretched his arm out behind him, finally losing her fingertips as the distance between them grew too great. Her arm fell to her side and Justin waved once as he climbed into the car.

Chandy remained rooted to the sidewalk, her lips quivering and nose running as Mrs. McCall backed out of the driveway. Justin gave her another sad wave, his face pressed to the glass as the car drove by. At the end of the block, the SUV made a turn on Cedar Street and disappeared from view.

It was the worst moment of her young life. As Chandy stood there shivering, she held on to the hope of dozens of letters and long-distance phone calls, the hope that somehow they'd bridge the gap. That their love would survive.

She never saw or heard from him again.

Chapter One

Fifteen years later

"Hush little baby, don't you cry…" Chandy McDaniel sang in a low voice as the runners of the wooden rocker made a rhythmic *thump, thump*. The two-month-old in her arms gave a soft sigh. Little Emily's lips puckered and Chandy put a finger to her own lips as Lynda entered the nursery. "Shh. She's finally asleep," Chandy whispered.

Lynda, a fiftysomething pediatric nurse with the St. Louis Crisis Nursery, nodded. "Good," she replied in the same hushed tone. "That little one's had a rough day. I thought she'd never settle down. But you always have the magic touch."

"Thanks." Chandy lowered her chin to gaze at the baby she'd cradled on her chest. Smooth skin and perfect tiny features hid the ugly truth. Little Emily's mother was temporarily unable to care for her daughter because her boyfriend had broken Emily's mom's arm the day before. So Emily had been brought here, to one of the five crisis-nursery locations in the St. Louis area. Chandy rocked more, unwilling to pass the infant over until she was certain Emily wouldn't stir. She'd been overly fussy today.

"You're so good with babies," Lynda observed, arms at her side but ready.

"Thanks." Chandy repeated, not breaking her rocking rhythm. Chandy had been volunteering at the nursery for the past two years, and her main duty was to hold and rock the youngest infants.

Finally convinced Emily wouldn't wake up, Chandy faced the inevitable, rose to her feet and handed the sweet-smelling baby to Lynda, who was working the night shift. "You leaving now?" Lynda asked.

Chandy nodded. "Yeah. Tomorrow's Sunday but I'm on E.R. duty starting at 7:00 a.m. You know it'll be busy. This weather's been far too nice. It's more like May than March and every weekend warrior will be outside overdoing it."

"Yeah, I couldn't believe that it hit ninety yesterday. I thought I'd need to turn on the air-conditioning it was so hot. Well, have a good night and I'll see you next time you come through."

"Definitely." Chandy retrieved her purse, signed out and headed for her car. The temperatures had been unusually warm all week. Tomorrow marked the last day of summerlike weather. The meteorologists predicted rain would move in Sunday evening and bring back the gray days, heavier coats and umbrellas that were typical for the end of winter.

As she stepped out into the balmy parking lot, Chandy reflected that St. Louis weather was insane, and even though she'd been living in the city for eight years, ever since she'd done her pediatric residency at Cardinal Glennon Children's Hospital, she'd never quite adjusted to the crazy temperature fluctuations.

However, she loved St. Louis, which was why she'd chosen to take a job as a pediatrician at West County Family Health instead of returning to Iowa. She enjoyed her job. The one minor downside was that she had shifts several times a month at the nearby hospital's pediatric E.R. with which the practice was affiliated. Working in the E.R. added extra hours to her week.

Traffic was light for a Saturday evening, and it didn't take long to get to her Kirkwood condo, a one-bedroom garden unit located off Ballas Road that she'd purchased because she liked the mature trees and friendly neighborhood setting. She parked in the garage and entered her apartment. Her cat, Mr. Wu, met her at the door and followed her into the kitchen, rubbing against her leg as she filled his empty food bowl.

She opened the fridge and removed the prepackaged Cobb salad she'd bought at the local supermarket the day before, then ate dinner while she checked Facebook on her laptop. Lisa needed a ball of twine in Mafia Wars. Jenny had announced she was pregnant again. Hope was going to Paris for two weeks. Chandy finished reading everyone's status updates but didn't post anything herself—her friends led much more interesting lives than she did. She didn't really mind, though. She'd never been the party-animal type, anyway.

She moved to close her browser, but before she could log out a chat icon popped up. Her older brother Chase was online. Eight years separated them, but after he'd become CEO of the family company and married his soul mate, they'd become even closer. What are you doing? he typed.

Just got home from the crisis nursery, she replied.

Ah.

She chewed a bite of her salad while the icon flashed, telling her he was typing something else. Chase would turn forty soon, and his and Miranda's three-year-old son, Bobby, was the cutest thing in the world.

The chat window flashed. Stop thinking about it.

Chandy leaned back in her chair and pushed her dinner aside, having lost her appetite. She'd actually been trying to avoid thinking about it, although she'd hadn't quite succeeded. While holding Emily she'd fought back quite a few tears. I'm not, she typed.

Liar, Chase returned.

Chandy sighed as Chase typed more. The high-speed connection brought his words quickly to the lower right corner of her laptop screen. It's been fifteen years. Let it go.

Chandy drummed her fingers on the table. Chase meant well, but he'd never understand. How could he? His son had been born healthy. Her child had died before it had become viable. Just a mass of cells growing inside her with no distinguishable features.

Yet she'd been devastated. She'd miscarried on March 5, and ever since, the first few days of March had been painful. She couldn't help herself. She grieved for what she'd lost—and for the children she'd never have.

Everyone thought that after fifteen years she should

be over her miscarriage. And the remainder of the year she sent the knowledge that she'd lost her baby and could never have another into the far recesses of her mind.

But every anniversary she mourned for what she'd lost. Her last therapist had said that her behavior was normal and for the first time, Chandy hadn't felt like a freak. After all, at that point she'd been holding on to the guilt for thirteen years.

I have to be up early for work. Talk to you later, she typed to Chase, suddenly unwilling to talk anymore, even to him. She logged out of Facebook and glanced at the clock. Not quite eight-thirty. Too soon for bed, and far too late to go do anything when she had to get up at 6:00 a.m. for work.

So here she sat on a Saturday night, alone, if she didn't count Mr. Wu. As if knowing he was needed, her fat black Persian jumped into her lap and began to purr.

Chandy scratched the cat behind his ears. If she'd kept talking to her brother she knew what he would have said. Now that he'd married and found the love of his life he was a regular matchmaker. He would've told her she should find a guy and settle down.

But how could she? She might marry, but marriage usually meant having kids, and the infection following her miscarriage had robbed her of that ability.

She'd also lost the last piece of Justin and the life she'd thought they'd have. While her grandfather had been supportive of Chandy and her decision to be a teenage mother, he'd seen the miscarriage as fate's way of giving her a fresh start. Although he'd tried not to show it, she knew he'd been relieved.

Chandy set Mr. Wu on the floor and went into the bathroom. She could do this. Maybe this could be the year she finally let go of the past. Ten years ago her then therapist had told her she had to face herself. She'd told Chandy to list all her positives, reaffirming her personal value. Chandy wasn't sure her advice worked, but as she did every year since the therapist's recommendation, she started reciting the list of her assets aloud.

"I'm a good doctor."

She sounded so stupid. She gripped the sink and forced herself not to look away from the image in the mirror. Taking a deep breath, she continued.

"I work out. I eat right. I'm smart."

The cat came in, sat and stared at her. "I am not crazy," she told him. He simply blinked.

She faced herself again and said the words that she always said but sometimes had a hard time believing. "I'm worthy. I'm a good person. It wasn't my fault. I can be a whole person without being able to give birth."

She repeated the final affirmations five times, fighting back the tears. Then she shook her head savagely, uttered a small curse and grabbed her toothbrush and the toothpaste tube. Scarlett O'Hara had declared that tomorrow was another day. Well, for Chandy tomorrow was D-day. She squared her chin. Like Scarlett, she would survive.

THE WILD PITCH THAT HIT Ben McCall in the side of the head was one of those freak accidents that just sort of happened. Combine warm weather, a dry field and a chance to get a two-week jump on the official start of freshman baseball practice, and Ben and his friends had been raring to go. They'd met at the local park, and the last thing the group of fourteen-year-old boys were concerned about was safety. After all, wearing those batting helmets sucked.

But they were necessary, as all discovered when the ball clocked Ben in the left temple and the impact dropped him to the ground like a rock.

Thirty-five minutes later, Ben's dad, Justin, had him at the pediatric E.R. of a west county hospital. After initial triage, someone installed Ben in an examination room where the nurse again took his vitals.

"He was unconscious on the field, but no one knows exactly how long. Thirty seconds? A minute?" Justin told her. He'd folded his six-foot frame into one of those black plastic chairs that were never comfortable. Today he'd planned on watching the NASCAR race and doing some laundry. He'd been petrified when he'd gotten the phone call that Ben was unconscious. Yet Ben had been awake by the time he'd arrived at the field.

The nurse finished the blood pressure check and gave Justin a benign, flat smile. "The doctor will be in shortly."

"Thanks." Justin leaned back, placing his head against the white wall. How many other fathers had stared up at the same white drop-tile ceiling? He lowered his eyes and gazed across the room. Ben lay on the hospital bed. His head obviously hurt, as he'd draped his arm across his eyes to keep out the light, and Justin could clearly see the huge ugly bruise that had formed on his temple.

"You doing okay?" Justin asked.

"Yeah," Ben replied, hardly moving.

Justin folded his hands into his lap. The waiting was always the hardest part. He'd been in the E.R. or urgent care with his son several times before. When Ben had been three he'd climbed on the toilet, reached for something, fallen, and bitten through his lip. That had required three stitches. When he'd fallen off his bike, that had been another nine. He'd broken his arm at age eight in a skateboarding accident, sprained his knee while playing soccer at ten. Otherwise he was a pretty healthy child. Lean. Muscular. Already five-eleven. Just a typical boy who everyone said looked like his dad.

Although, Justin did see a hint of his ex-wife. Ben had Lorna's lips and smile. He had her intelligence, but thankfully not her propensity to waste it. Ben had gotten straight As in middle school, although he hadn't had to apply himself much. He was finding high school to be a lot harder, and Justin prayed that Ben would continue to do well. So far his son's grades had been good. Grades were important—Justin wanted Ben to go to college and make something of himself. He wanted his son to be able to be more than just the owner of an auto body repair shop.

Sure, being a business owner provided a decent living and Justin enjoyed his work. He also had good health insurance, and some money set aside for retirement and Ben's college tuition. But his life wasn't supposed to have turned out this way, and he wanted Ben to have the choices he hadn't had.

The knob turned and the door began to open. A blonde doctor dressed in a white jacket entered. Her name was stitched over her heart, but Justin would have known her anywhere, even after fifteen years. He fought back the surprise as her name returned to his lips. "Chandy?"

AT THE FAMILIAR USE OF her name, Chandy's head turned toward the man who unfolded himself from the uncomfortable plastic chair. She'd entered the exam room, her focus on the teenage boy lying on the bed. Ben McCall, according to the charts. A common enough name.

Wrong.

She felt herself sway a little. What was the probability? And on March 5 of all days? One in a trillion?

Fate had to be mocking her, for the man in the room was none other than a grown-up version of the gangly boy with the shaggy hair who had left her standing on the sidewalk in the cold.

Yet he'd changed…and not for the worse. He'd become a well-built man with a handsome face. His blue eyes were the same and as they had in high school, even after fifteen years, they automatically made her knees weak. "Justin?"

"Chandy. It is you."

"Yes." She took a deep breath and found her poise. Recovered. After all, a decade and a half was a long time. She was no longer the naive girl who'd loved him and lost his baby. She was no longer the desperate and depressed girl who'd waited for letters and phone calls that had never come.

She moved to the bed and concentrated on work. She was experienced in dealing with trauma, and that included her own. She could handle this turn of events. She would handle the situation, and with grace. She kept her voice light. "So, Ben, I hear you got hit with a baseball."

"Yeah. Petey throws a mean fastball." Ben's joke was accompanied by a wince.

"And you weren't wearing a batting helmet," she stated, more for his benefit than anything. She already knew the answer, which was obvious from the bruising and lump on his head.

"Learned that lesson the hard way," Ben mumbled.

"Yes, you did. Well, let me take a look." She lifted his arm and did a quick visual examination. "So how old are you?"

"Fourteen."

"Freshman?"

"Uh-huh. I can't miss baseball season. It starts soon."

He blinked, and she saw that he had his father's eyes. Would her child have had those baby blues had he or she survived? She calmed herself, refusing to get further rattled, and continued her exam. "I'm sure I can get you patched up by then. But once I do it's a helmet from here on out for all sports. No exceptions. Ever."

"Okay. Can I go to sleep now?"

"Touch your nose for me," she said. Ben tried and missed.

"Touch your fingertip to mine." Ben had trouble making the connections as Chandy moved her hand and had him repeat the process.

She stepped back a few feet and turned to Justin. "I'm ordering a CT scan. I'd like a picture of what's going on inside his head."

Justin nodded. "Okay."

"They'll be in shortly to come get him." With that Chandy turned, grabbed the doorknob and got herself out of there before he could ask her anything else.

"You look like you've seen a ghost," Dr. Paige Walter remarked as Chandy returned to the nurses' station. At forty, Paige was a pediatric plastic surgeon. Over the past two years she and Chandy had become good friends.

"Big ghost actually. A former high school boyfriend. And his son."

A son who was fourteen. She kept the angry tremble from her hand. So much for Justin's telling her she'd always have his heart and all those other lies... No wonder he'd lost contact. He certainly hadn't wasted much time replacing her and knocking up someone else, had he?

"You can get Bryan to take over," Paige suggested. Bryan was one of the other pediatricians working the E.R. that day, and because of the great weather, as they'd expected, they were swamped with kids who'd injured themselves while playing outside.

Chandy processed the CT order. "We're too busy

for me to shuffle this off on him. Besides, I can handle seeing Justin."

Paige appeared scandalized. "I wouldn't do it. Pass it over."

"It's fine. It was fifteen years ago. It's not like we were married or he treated me terribly. He just moved to a different town. Things happen." Chandy shrugged, presenting an indifferent front.

Paige's skepticism faded at Chandy's reassurances. "Okay. If you're sure. Oh, and while I'm remembering, Craig wants to ask you out."

Craig was an anesthesiologist and a friend of Paige's husband. Chandy had met Craig a few weeks ago at a mutual colleague's birthday party. Craig was thirty-seven, and a nice guy although a bit introverted. Seeing the hopeful look on Paige's face, Chandy sighed and caved. After all, it had been a month or two since her last date. "I'll go. But just one and it has to be a double with you and Ahmed. How about dinner? And a movie, but only if things go well."

Paige grinned. "That'll work. And don't worry. Craig's great. I'll set it up and text you."

"Sounds like a plan."

"Chandy, your X-ray report just came up from Radiology," one of the nurses told her.

"Thanks." Ensured Ben was now in the queue for his CT scan, Chandy pressed a button on the computer, read the radiologist's report, looked at the digital images that clearly showed the broken bone, and then went off to tell a seven-year-old he was going to wear a cast on his arm for the next six weeks.

EVER SINCE THEY'D WHEELED Ben off to Radiology, Justin had been sitting alone in the examination room. When he'd left for the hospital he should have grabbed a book or something, but he hadn't thought of that in his hurry to load Ben into the car. So he waited in silence, consumed by his thoughts. Chandy McDaniel. The last person he'd ever expected to see again.

He leaned his head against the wall and closed his eyes. He'd hated what he'd had to do, but when he'd gotten to Chicago, he'd known it was best to break things off.

Oh, he'd never wanted to stop seeing her. How many times had he dialed her number, reaching the last digit before hanging up? For months he'd thought of her every day. He'd started hundreds of letters, but then he'd thrown them away.

For really, what was there to say? He couldn't tell her the truth. That he hated Chicago. That he'd gone from a nice house in a good neighborhood to the best his mom could afford. That his younger brother, Derek, acted up constantly and that Justin always had to get him out of messes. Worse, his uncle was far more interested in drinking beer than raising his sister's boys. His promise of support was the reason his mother had moved in the first place. The extra adult help she'd hoped for hadn't materialized, so Justin had had to grow up fast.

He'd known he couldn't leave and return to Chandy. Not when his mother needed him. Despite all of his feelings, he'd recognized it was best to let Chandy go.

Besides, he hadn't wanted her pity. She would have wanted to try to fix things. She was Chandy McDaniel, a member of Chenille's first family and granddaughter of the richest man in town. She believed that she could do anything.

Yet in the seamier side of Chicago, seventeen-year-old Justin had learned the truth—there was nothing anyone could do. His fate had been sealed when his mom had pulled out of the driveway and left Chenille behind. At that moment, his life had taken a decidedly different turn.

In Chenille, Justin had concentrated solely on school, sports and Chandy. In Chicago he'd gotten a job at the local grocery store and helped with the bills. School sucked since he knew no one, and his dream of playing baseball faded under the pressures of trying to manage Derek. He hadn't attended prom and his ball glove had grown dusty. He'd traded college applications for a job fixing up cars. So despite all her letters, which had dwindled as time marched on, he'd severed contact.

After all, he was no longer living the dream they'd shared. In the back of his mind he'd always known he wasn't good enough for the granddaughter of McDaniel Manufacturing's CEO. But Leroy McDaniel had tolerated him because Justin made Chandy happy. And in small-town Chenille, if the granddaughter of the CEO said Justin was worthy, well, then he was. Sure it helped that he was a star athlete. Chenille rewarded potential and hard work, not social class. Yet in Chicago he was just another face in a school where no one cared.

Justin glanced around the room, noting all the equipment about which he had no clue. Chandy would, though. Here she was, fifteen years later, the one in charge. She'd become a doctor. She'd mentioned medical school once, but hadn't seriously considered that career path since they'd had their life together all planned out.

Now Justin took some comfort in knowing that once he'd left she'd been free to pursue a passion, to do something beyond just working for McDaniel until becoming a stay-at-home mom.

Fifteen years later, Justin knew that dreams like the one he and Chandy had shared weren't real. All life gave you was obstacles, and perhaps, with enough hard work, you might be able to achieve your goals.

He'd busted his tail to get out of Chicago and make a decent life for himself and his son, but seeing Chandy today proved he'd never be on the same playing field as her. She lived in a white-collar, professional world. He was blue-collar, dirty hands. Chandy's crowd could afford to shop at high-end specialty stores; he shopped at Wal-Mart.

An orderly opened the door and rolled the hospital bed back inside. Justin rose to his feet and went to Ben's side. "Hey. You okay? How was it?"

"My head still hurts. But the machine was kind of cool. I just lay there and the bed moved. Kinda hot around my nose, though."

Justin hated to see his son in pain. "Well, we should know what's going on when the doctor returns."

Ben dropped his arm back across his face. "You called her Chandy."

"I knew her in high school," Justin admitted.

"Which one?" Ben asked.

"Chenille. Before I moved to Chicago. A very long time ago."

"Oh." Ben yawned. The blow had made him sleepy, and Justin went back to his chair to let the boy rest.

About fifteen minutes later, Justin heard a knock on the door and Chandy reappeared. "He's asleep," Justin told her.

She didn't appear concerned. "That's fine. We used to have to keep concussion victims awake, but these days with the CT scan we can see exactly what's going on."

"So what is going on?" Justin asked. Seeing Chandy in professional mode was fascinating. There was a confidence about her that he liked. The shoulder-length blond hair he remembered as being soft and silky was pinned up into a bun. Her face was rounder and her lips fuller. She'd matured and come into her own—she was a very desirable woman. He noticed that she wasn't wearing a wedding ring.

"Ben has a concussion. However, the CT scan shows no internal bleeding or swelling, which is excellent news as it means we don't need to keep him for observation. The only real treatment now is rest. I don't want him exerting himself for at least a week. No P.E. or baseball for two weeks, not even a light game or tossing a ball with friends. For the pain he can have acetaminophen, but do not give him any ibuprofen tablets or any type of anti-inflammatory drugs. Those can increase the risk of bleeding."

"Okay," Justin replied, absorbing everything she was telling him.

"You'll get a treatment plan before he's discharged.

You'll need to watch for postconcussion syndrome. Follow up with your family pediatrician if there are severe headaches, forgetfulness and dizziness that continue after a week. If Ben seems listless or off balance, or if he starts vomiting, those are other signs to get him checked out. He might also be more irritable, stubborn or anxious."

"Those last ones are normal states with him." His jest failed to earn a smile from her. Chandy was all business.

"Really, if he takes care of himself, wears a helmet for every sport and doesn't injure his head again, he should be fine. Multiple concussions are dangerous."

Justin nodded soberly. "Understood."

Her lips thinned into one of those pleasant yet impatient smiles that people give when they're dying to escape. "Great. I'll send in a nurse to provide detailed instructions and the paperwork you need to sign."

As Chandy moved to leave, Justin reached out to stop her. He touched her sleeve, and as she paused, he yanked his hand back. "Chandy."

Her fingers hovered above the doorknob. "Yes?"

"How are you?"

"Busy. Lots of patients today. No time to chat." She was blowing him off. Yet even though time had passed, some things never changed, and he could tell that deep down she was mad at him. He knew he deserved her anger—he'd cut her off without telling her why.

"Look, could we maybe meet for coffee and talk? Just as old friends? I owe you an explanation."

She averted her eyes. "I'm not sure that's a good idea. I doubt your wife would approve."

"I'm divorced."

She gazed at him then, her mouth parting slightly, reminding him of how soft her lips had always felt. "Oh. Sorry to hear that."

"It's okay." He'd rattled her. Some of the professionalism she'd wrapped around herself like a shield had slipped, revealing raw vulnerability. Realization socked him in the gut. He'd truly hurt her. Terribly.

His actions at seventeen had been selfish. He'd told himself that he was protecting her, but in truth he'd been ashamed and embarrassed by his life in Chicago. He'd rationalized that she'd get over him, but he'd underestimated her. He was a jerk of the highest order.

"I'd like a chance to explain. To apologize. I owe you that."

She shook her head. "It's all in the past. We need to leave it behind us. I'm fine."

He reached into his jeans pocket, removed a business card from his wallet and held it out. To his relief she took it. "If you change your mind, call me. I'm also on Facebook. You can find me in the St. Louis network."

"Sure." He could tell she was itching to go. "It was nice seeing you. Your son will be fine." She opened the door and with a swish of white coat, left him standing there.

The nurse appeared shortly to repeat Chandy's instructions and add a few more, and about fifteen minutes later, Justin had Ben loaded into the car. He glanced behind him at the hospital. Dr. Chandy McDaniel—as beautiful as ever.

Running into her had been a blow. A reminder of how many mistakes he'd made. He consoled himself with the fact that he had Ben, who was the best thing he'd ever done, even if his conception had been accidental. Justin drove off knowing he wouldn't hear from Chandy again.

CHANDY CARRIED THE BUSINESS card around inside her pants pocket, not removing the card until after she'd reached her condo that night and had microwaved herself a TV dinner.

She stirred the lemon chicken and linguine around in the black plastic dish and wrinkled her nose. She should be starving, but food held no appeal for her tonight. Sighing, she picked up Justin's business card.

"McCall Auto Body in Eureka, MO. Specializing in high-end restorations. Justin McCall, owner."

While he'd liked cars in high school and had dreamed of restoring a 1960s muscle car, she never would have expected him to own a repair shop. Then again, people changed.

He'd always been attractive, but at thirty-two he was downright hot. His face had been covered with light stubble, and she'd ached to feel the texture. His hands had been weathered and worn, and she wondered if he still had the same soft, gentle touch. His hair hadn't grayed, and his full lips curved in a warm smile. And his eyes. Those baby blues had always seen through her. He'd known she didn't want to talk.

She reached for her laptop, fired it up and gave in to her curiosity. Logging into her Facebook account, she immediately typed his name in the search feature. His picture appeared at the top of the list, with two mutual friends—people they'd known in high school who Chandy had added as friends but really didn't talk to anymore. That was the beauty of Facebook. You could know everyone's daily business and never see the person once.

She clicked on Justin's profile. She studied his wall, and then clicked on his information. Relationship status: Divorced. Birthday: September 30. Favorite band: Goo Goo Dolls. She loved them, too.

She followed his work history from the first auto body shop in Chicago to his opening his own place in St. Louis.

How ironic that somehow they'd made it to the same city. Even more odd was running into him, especially as she'd been in St. Louis for a long time.

Fate could be interesting. Perhaps this was a cosmic sign she'd wallowed long enough. If Justin moved on, so should she.

She clicked on Justin's photos and wasn't surprised to see that most of them were of Ben. There was Ben fishing. Ben driving a go-kart. Ben playing baseball. There were some of Ben and Justin together. A few of Ben and his grandmother, Justin's mom.

It was obvious how much Justin loved his son. Clearly Justin's marriage hadn't ended well—the hospital paperwork had indicated he had sole custody. She allowed herself some bittersweet regret. Justin had always told her they'd be married forever. He hadn't believed in divorce. Obviously he did now.

Chandy clicked the *X* in the corner and closed the laptop cover. She'd been foolish to look at his profile. Now the hole in her heart had opened far too wide. Justin had gotten married shortly after high school, judging from Ben's age. No wonder Justin had never called or written—he'd met someone else. All the love that had burned inside her, that love which had died a slow, painful death as months went by, had meant nothing to him. Nothing at all.

She could finally see the wisdom of her grandfather's actions all those years ago. When she'd found out she was pregnant, she'd immediately wanted to call Justin and tell him about the baby. She was certain he'd have come home to Chenille to be with her.

But her grandfather had suggested she wait. Her parents had died when she was extremely young, so Leroy was like a father to her. Although she had protested his insistence not to tell Justin, she had trusted him. In the end, she'd bowed to his wishes, and after she'd miscarried, there had been no point.

Seeing Justin and Ben today had told her she had been young and naive. He wouldn't have come for her. He hadn't loved her. Her grandfather had been right all along.

She picked up the business card and, with savage determination, ripped it in two and threw it away.

Chapter Two

Three weeks later, Chandy tapped her fingers on the steering wheel of her Jag. She kept time to the music, which was about all she could do as she was sitting in bumper-to-bumper traffic on Ballas Road, waiting patiently for the light at Manchester to change. Traffic was always heavy during afternoon rush hour when the southbound lanes of Highway 270 crawled and frustrated drivers took to the side roads in droves.

She'd tried not to think of Justin, and had even joined some colleagues for a little St. Patrick's Day revelry. Although March 21 had come and gone on the calendar, the sunny weather and springlike days had vanished. Instead thick gray clouds loomed overhead, an inch of snow threatened, and the heater blasted to keep out the chill.

She crept forward another two feet and stopped again. The taller concrete buildings of the Edward Jones headquarters dwarfed the bare trees ahead and beyond those was the mall—she was almost home. The five-mile commute was going to take twenty minutes today.

She had her third date with Craig tonight, but because

of a flu epidemic and a full schedule she was running an hour behind and had already rescheduled their meeting time once. At this rate they weren't going to make the 7:00 p.m. movie.

Sadly, she didn't care. Craig was a nice guy, but after two dates it had become painfully clear there wasn't any real chemistry between them. And worse, Craig couldn't compare to Justin.

She drummed her fingers on the steering wheel, now out of frustration. Seeing him had put her into a deep funk. It had almost broken her heart all over again to learn she'd been so easily replaced. And she couldn't believe her traitorous body was still attracted to the man who had caused her so much—

The loud bang from behind was echoed by one from the front, and followed by a split second of incomprehension as smoke filled the car. All she saw was a white cloud as her neck jerked and her body smacked the air bag.

The car hood crumpled toward her, and the air bag launched the arm holding the steering wheel back toward her chest.

Then all was still. Her surroundings came into focus as the air bag accelerant dissipated. The engine had died; the car was stopped. She turned the key—nothing. She put the car in Park and tried again. Still nothing. Unsure what to do, she attempted to wedge her door open. Failing, she climbed out the other side. She rubbed her neck, which was tender.

Already people had gotten out of their cars to help, and as the fire station was across from the mall, she could hear the approaching sirens. The teenage boy driving the SUV that had hit her approached, fear and worry obvious. "I'm so sorry. I thought you were moving. I hit the gas too hard. Are you okay?"

"Yeah." Chandy shivered and rubbed the back of her neck again. She'd diagnosed enough cases to know she had whiplash.

The Des Peres police arrived quickly and directed the cars be moved to the shoulder. A female officer interviewed for the accident report. After making her statement, Chandy dialed Paige and told her friend what had happened. "I need a flatbed and a repair shop."

"Let me get the number of the guy we used when our Porsche got hit. Hold on." Paige came back on the line a second later. "Got a pen? Here's the towing company we like. Osthoff's. Call them and have them take your car to McCall's in Eureka."

"McCall's?" Chandy echoed as she wrote down the towing company's number. She knew that last name far too well and this time knew exactly who owned the place. "They're that good?"

"The best body shop in town. We've used them on two cars now. One was Ahmed's classic Camaro, which cost us a fortune to restore, but you've seen the results. Beautiful. The other was the Porsche. Ahmed won't go anywhere else."

"Okay. Thanks. I've got to go. Wait." Chandy winced. "Do me a favor. Call Craig and cancel for me. I'm not up for going anywhere tonight."

"Of course not. You need rest. I'll let him know

and you take care of yourself. Call me if you need anything."

"I will." Chandy hung up as the paramedics came to look her over. Wanting just to go home, she promised to take herself to the E.R. later if her pain increased. Then she called the towing company; they told her someone would be there shortly.

The female officer returned. "The SUV driver is clearly at fault for both your car and the one you hit. He has insurance—here's the information. You'll need to contact his insurance company and file a claim. Most insurers take claims 24/7."

"I will. Can you recommend someplace to have the repair work done? I've never been in an accident."

The officer glanced at Chandy's car. "I used McCall's when someone rear-ended me and I drive a three-year-old Malibu. For your car, McCall's will be the best. They do good work at fair prices. Tell the towing company and they'll store your car and take it over first thing Monday."

So two recommendations for Justin's shop, and one was from a complete stranger. While she would prefer to avoid Justin, she wanted her car fixed right. It was only three months old, a gift she's bought herself for Christmas as her previous car had been on its last legs. Now her dream car was crumpled.

The flatbed arrived, and the driver loaded the Jag, ready to cart it off. "Where is it going?" he asked.

Chandy shivered. She'd made her decision. "Take it to McCall's."

"Good choice. They'll have this baby in tip-top shape in no time."

She sighed, understanding the implications of her actions. She'd have to see Justin again.

THINGS AT MCCALL'S WERE already in full swing when Justin arrived around eight Monday morning. The shop had opened at seven, although Justin never arrived until after he'd fed Ben breakfast and seen the taillights of the school bus as it drove away.

In eighth grade, when Justin had trusted his son to get himself up, Ben had missed the bus far too many times. So now Justin did the fifteen-minute drive to work after Ben left.

"So what have we got?" Justin asked his office manager, Shelley.

She pushed a brown hair off her face. "Osthoff Towing dropped off two cars. A Cadillac CTS and a Jaguar XK. Both are direct repair accident insurance jobs, although not the same accident or company. I haven't gotten ahold of the CTS owner yet, but I've spoken with the Jag owner. I made sure she was okay. Said she was sore all weekend but that she's fine. I've got her claim number."

She gave him a pink message slip. "She says she knows you and asked to talk to you when you had a moment."

Justin's eyebrows arched as he read the name on the paper in his hand. His fingers shook as he shoved the paper into his jeans pocket. Chandy had been in a wreck? He calmed himself. Shelley had said she was okay. He tried to relax, but suddenly his breakfast wasn't sitting well. "She has a nice car."

"The current year model. I saw it. It's loaded. What bad luck. She was rear-ended and shoved into the car in front. Her car took damage on both ends." Shelley reached for the ringing phone.

"I'll go take a look." Justin grabbed a cup of coffee and strolled onto the shop floor. When he'd first gotten started back in Chicago, he'd been one of the guys out there doing the hands-on repair.

When his dream of college had died, he'd discovered he was good at bodywork. In Chenille he'd loved to tinker with cars, and he'd been able to turn his hobby into a living. Ten years ago he'd met a man looking to sell his body shop, but the place was in St. Louis. Still, it had been the chance of a lifetime and Justin had invested his meager savings and gotten a small business loan. After a lot of hard work, his investment had paid off.

While he still got his hands dirty, it was far less now that he owned the place. Mostly he oversaw repairs, did estimates, ordered parts and scheduled work.

"Nice job, Lou," he said as he stopped by a Mustang getting final touches. The owner had hit an eight-point buck and the entire front end had looked as if someone had taken a pointed ice cream scoop to the hood and grill. Tomorrow the car would be painted, and by Friday, the owner could drive it home.

As he did every morning, Justin assessed the workload. His shop floor was full. He had multiple insurance jobs and three custom jobs for wealthy car enthusiasts.

Steve was working on a dream car—a 1960 Corvette whose owner called every day—it was a gift for his wife and he wanted to make sure it would be ready for their thirtieth anniversary. Justin had assured him it would. The work was coming along beautifully.

Justin made his way outside, ignoring the brisk air as he stepped into the fenced lot where wrecked cars awaited their turn on the shop floor. He saw the CTS, which didn't appear to be too terribly beaten up. It would need a new hood, front bumper and alignment… He began a mental list. Then he came to the Jaguar and winced.

The aluminum body had crumpled. The back had dented inward from the impact, and the front had peeled open, the hood forming a tent over the engine.

He sipped his coffee and tugged open the driver side door, which creaked and moaned, indicating the car's frame had buckled. The acrid smell of deployed air bags wafted out. He shut the door and returned to his office. After he warmed up, he'd put on his coat and go back outside to make notes on both cars. He'd send estimates to the adjusters, who would determine if the cars were to be repaired or totaled. Knowing the business as well as he did, though, Justin already knew these two were going to be repaired, so he'd make a list of parts to order and get started on that.

First, even though Shelley had spoken with Chandy, Justin always spoke with his clients himself. It was something he'd learned from his first boss—to be accessible and caring. After all, he knew that after accidents clients were shaken and often unfamiliar with what happened next.

And in Chandy's case he had more than professional concern...

As CHANDY SAID GOODBYE to her patient and headed for the next room, one of the nurses stopped her. "Chandy, you have a phone call. Justin from the body shop is on line two."

Chandy glanced down the hall at the row of examination rooms, all with waiting patients in various stages of processing. "You can take five minutes without getting too backed up," the nurse said.

"All right." Chandy hurried to her office and sat down. She calmed her nerves and pressed the button for line two. "Dr. McDaniel."

"It's Justin."

His smooth, sexy baritone washed over her, sending an unwelcome tingle of awareness down to her toes. "How's my car?" she asked.

"Well, we're going to make it as good as new."

She hadn't really needed to talk to him, and now, as she gripped the black handset, she wondered why she'd left a message at all. The kid had a high enough insurance maximum to cover all repairs. She had nothing to worry about.

"How are you?" Justin asked.

"Fine." Chandy swiveled toward the windows as a different nurse walked by the open doorway, en route to a patient room.

"No leftover soreness from the impact?"

Oh, that was what he'd meant. She shouldn't be so rattled. She'd slept most of the weekend. "Some tightness but it's fading. No real problems."

"Good. The car's pretty crunched up and I was worried about you."

"Well, it's nothing that some acetaminophen can't fix." She tugged on the cord. "Do you have an estimate on how long it'll take to get my car back?"

"Four weeks minimum, eight maximum."

She frowned. "That long?"

"It'll take at least a week for parts to get here. You don't have a common car. We use only genuine replacement parts, and these things aren't just lying around."

She exhaled. "Okay. Sorry. I do want my car fixed right."

"Don't worry. Your frustration is normal. Accidents are traumatic for anyone, but you'll bounce back. You always did, and you couldn't have changed that much."

Oh, but she had. She'd grown up, gotten wiser. Cried rivers of tears over the family she'd never have.

She glanced over her shoulder at the doorway again. Empty, meaning she had a little more time before her patient load backed up and she got off schedule.

"Can I see the car? If possible I'd like to retrieve some things. When I got home I realized I hadn't cleaned out the trunk. I've got stuff back there that I need."

"Sure. Today is fine. We're open until six."

"I have patients until four. I should be able to be there by closing time."

"Call me on my cell if you can't. I can keep the place open. Do you still have my card?"

"No."

He didn't seem surprised but instead rattled off a number, and she scrambled for a pen and paper to write it down. "I'll see you later tonight," she said.

Chandy arrived at the body shop around a quarter to six. She'd looked up the location on MapQuest, so she found the nondescript building easily. She parked and went inside; the main waiting area was pleasant and the receptionist desk empty. A wall of glass lined one wall, and behind were cars in various stages of repair. The place was empty.

She turned as she heard a rustle, and saw Ben coming out of an office door. "Hi."

"Hey," he said. "Come to see about your car? My dad told me that was your Jag out there."

"It is and I have. How are you?"

He shrugged. "Fine."

Typical teenage answer. "No headaches? Dizziness?" Chandy pressed.

"Nope." He sat at the desk. "Did you know your first name is the same as Jimmie Johnson's wife?"

Chandy had no idea who he was talking about. "Who?"

"NASCAR driver. Three-time champion. Back to back." He pointed.

Chandy noticed for the first time the poster hanging on the wall. "No, I didn't know that. Interesting. Is your dad here?"

"Yeah. He's on the phone. So Dad says your car is brand-new."

She nodded. "I gave it to myself for Christmas. You should have seen what I drove before. It was pretty old."

"You bought a sweet ride. I looked the specs up on the Internet. You even have the azure metallic paint and the premium sound. I bet that's kick-butt."

"It is." Chandy replied, although she hadn't yet blasted the stereo.

"Have you topped it out yet?"

Her eyebrows knit together, unsure what he meant. "Huh?"

"Seen how fast it goes," Ben explained.

"I didn't buy it for that."

"That's because you're a girl," Ben supplied.

Chandy stared at him. "Really?"

"Yeah. A guy would want to know." He shrugged. "Well, don't worry. It'll get fixed. My dad's the best."

She could tell Ben wasn't bragging. "That's what everyone who recommended him says," Chandy replied.

"It's true." Ben turned his attention back to the computer.

Justin strolled out of the office then. He wore a long-sleeve red flannel shirt and blue jeans. "Hey, you made it."

"Yes, but I don't see my car." She pointed to the wall of glass.

"Oh, it won't be out there until we start work. Your car is in my storage lot. Follow me."

He opened a door and they cut across the shop floor.

He flipped a light switch before they exited into a large fenced yard. "There she is."

A blast of icy air whirled around Chandy as she approached her car. The floodlights had illuminated the Jaguar, showing her the full extent of the smashup. She circled the car slowly. "Wow. I saw them put it on the truck, but…"

"You were on an adrenaline high from the impact. Everyone says that it's amazing when you see the damage later."

"I'll say. I climbed out of that." Her car was a dented and lumpy mess. She touched her throat, extremely grateful to be alive. Things could have been so much worse. She trembled slightly.

He'd come up behind her. "Your car kept you safe. The car frame absorbed the impact as it was designed to do."

She touched the cold metal with bare fingertips. "There's so much damage."

"That's because the frame on your car is aluminum, which means it bends and gives more."

"That's why the insurance premium was higher."

He laughed. "What'd you drive before?"

"A six-year-old Toyota Camry that I'd driven into oblivion. When I went car shopping I decided I wanted something more fun, something upscale and sporty. I did some research and bought this."

"It's a great car. My son's been lusting over it all day. Don't worry, he's not old enough to drive. Although I might let him sit in it." He grinned. "Just kidding."

"No, it'd be fine. But yeah, better not let him take it on the road. He wanted to know how fast it goes."

"That sounds like Ben." Justin chuckled, and his smile lit up his face. Chandy's stomach gave a little flutter.

"Has he been wearing his batting helmet?" she asked, focusing on something professional and tamping her wayward emotions. She was only here for her car.

Justin's warm smile faded and he nodded, back to business himself. "Daily. His coach is all over those boys. Since Ben's head injury, he keeps telling them he doesn't want another accident on his watch."

"Good."

Justin reached into his pocket and withdrew her keyless remote. He unlocked the door and the trunk. "Now you can get your stuff."

Which was her real purpose. Being on his turf had sidetracked her, as had seeing him in his environment. He'd become quite the man—a successful business owner and devoted father.

She tugged open the passenger door, bent down and sniffed. The caramel-colored seats stank. In fact, everything did. "Ugh. Tell me that smell comes out."

"It does. Don't worry. It'll be as fresh as a new car when you get it back."

"Thank goodness." She grabbed her sunglasses and the garage-door remote, and put both in her purse. "I couldn't believe how bad my clothes reeked when I got home. I threw away my purse, it was so disgusting."

"It's a horrible stench, and I'm used to it. But it means

the air bags deployed and that you're safe. A small price to pay."

He had a point. "True."

He followed her around to the trunk and lifted the warped metal. She reached in, withdrew two shopping bags and balanced them on the crumpled bumper. "I'm probably going to have to wash all of this."

She took out a pink sleeper with the price tag still attached and sniffed. A whiff of a snowsuit indicated the same smell had permeated the fabric. "Yep. Laundry for everything."

He'd tilted his head slightly. "Do you have kids?"

She slid the bags onto her forearm and closed the trunk lid, which didn't fit well.

"Just leave that," Justin said. "That's getting fixed, too. So are those for your kids?"

"I don't have children." Her words came out brisk and matter-of-fact. "I'm donating these to the crisis nursery where I volunteer. They'll give the clothes to needy families."

"That's generous. Although I have no idea what you're talking about."

She warmed to her topic. "The crisis nursery is a place where parents who are in crisis can safely bring their children and leave them temporarily. The children are every age from infants on up, and the family gets all sorts of help. I like shopping for the newborn to two-year-olds. Baby clothes are cute. Didn't you love dressing up Ben? Didn't your ex enjoy it?"

Justin's lips turned downward. "She didn't stay around long—less than a year. I raised Ben on my own, and I was much more utilitarian than fashion-conscious. Now I just give him a prepaid Visa card and he picks out his own stuff. We have a deal that if I don't like it, he has to take it back."

"Oh. I see. Sorry, I didn't mean to pry."

She was such an idiot. He was going to repair her car, nothing more. She didn't need to be curious, or get involved, yet here she was, doing just that.

"Hey, it's fine. I told you I owed you an explanation. Especially about Ben."

"No, you really don't. Children are a blessing. No matter what the circumstances are." She turned her back on Justin and walked toward the door, not wanting to talk anymore.

She felt his presence right behind her. "Chandy."

She already had both feet on the first step, and this brought her to equal height with him as he put his hand on her shoulder. Her breath caught in her throat and she exhaled, the cold creating a small misty white cloud. "Justin, don't."

He held up his hands in surrender. "Don't what? Apologize? When I moved I said I'd write and call and I didn't do either. I was a total tool."

Any apology he gave would be too little, too late. The past couldn't be undone. Some things could never be repaired.

She shrugged, unwilling to let him know how much the entire situation wounded her. "We were young. Just stupid, foolish dreamers without a clue about how the real world worked. Life goes on. You've got Ben, and I've got a busy career."

Her cell phone beeped with a text message as if to confirm that.

"Maybe I have to explain. Make things right. Do you know how much guilt I've carried?"

Her forehead creased and she struggled for calm. She found that place inside herself where she could hide, where she could shut down all emotions. "What? Why is this so important? Are you doing twelve steps or something?" Her words sounded cold, harsh.

"No, and I deserve your anger." He paused. "Then again, perhaps it's sort of like that. Derek's been sober for five years."

She remembered Derek. He'd always been a rabble-rouser. "Good for him."

"Good for all of us. He put my mom through hell. He was constantly suspended from school for being in fights. He didn't stop drinking or creating chaos until he got the DWI. Luckily when he got probation instead of jail, he finally straightened himself out and got clean and sober."

Her fingers curled. Poor Mrs. McCall. Poor Justin for having to be the father figure for his brother. "I thought your uncle was going to help out."

"He did little."

"I'm sorry. I didn't know."

Justin's face had darkened. "No, you didn't, because I didn't want you to worry. I couldn't write or call and pretend that all was well. I didn't want to lie. Not to you."

Her lips quivered as her control snapped. "You could have just told me the truth. At least one letter. You could have had the decency to tell me why you were saying goodbye." Her last words came out in an angry rush.

His eyes didn't leave hers and she could see the sadness in them. "You're a fixer, Chandy. You like to make things better, and there was nothing you could do."

"You don't know that. Maybe I could have done something."

He shook his head. "I thought I was protecting you. It was hopeless."

"All I wanted to do was understand what happened. A harsh goodbye would have been better than not knowing! Better than silence. Better than..." *being alone when I lost the baby.*

Her chest constricted and she took several gulps of air as she tried to compose herself. "There is no point in rehashing what went wrong fifteen years ago. Let's just leave things alone, let them be. When my car's done we'll go our separate ways. It's a big city. After all, we've never run into each other before." She pivoted and yanked the door open.

She strode inside and headed for the waiting area. She heard Justin curse as he locked the door and hit the light switch. "Chandy."

"I'll talk to you later, Justin."

She opened the door to the lobby. Ben lounged at the desk, surfing the Internet. "You going?" he asked.

She didn't stop walking. "Yes."

"Bye," Ben called, his face readable. He sensed her tension.

So she paused at the exterior door, seeing a young version of Justin, at about the same age as he'd been when she'd first fallen in love. Goodbyes were so important. "You keep wearing that helmet, okay?"

"Okay. I will." He smiled and her heart broke.

"Goodbye." She pulled the door open and walked out into the night.

FROM THE TENSE SCRUNCH of her shoulders, Justin knew better than to follow Chandy. Chasing after her would only make things worse. He remembered how stubborn she could be.

"She seemed in a hurry to leave," Ben remarked, his gaze never leaving the computer screen, as Justin entered the waiting room.

"Yeah. She had places to be." Justin tried to sound casual.

"So were you friends in high school?" Ben asked, fingers moving the mouse.

"You could say that."

Ben's phone beeped and he grabbed it and checked his text message. His thumbs immediately began typing a reply, and Justin knew he'd lost interest in the Chandy conversation. Thank goodness.

As for Justin, he and Chandy weren't done talking. Perhaps it was like those twelve steps. For a short time he and his mother had joined a support group for those who lived with alcoholics, so Justin had learned the steps. Although he'd gone to the meetings specifically to find out how to deal with his brother, the skills he'd learned also applied to what was happening with Chandy. He'd wronged her. Now that he finally realized how badly, he needed to make amends, for both his own peace of mind and hers.

What he didn't understand was why she seemed so afraid to face the past.

Seeing her again had brought everything back. Justin believed that nothing was ever mere coincidence. Ben's head injury and Chandy's car accident were fate's way of giving him a chance to make things right. To say he was sorry. To remove the terrible burden of regret and uncertainty that had weighed on him for fifteen years. From her reaction to him today, he knew that all was not well in Chandy's world, either. He owed it to her to make things right.

Justin reached into his pocket and withdrew the keys. He would see her again. After all, he had her car.

Chapter Three

"So when is your car going to be done?" Paige asked, lifting the bottle of beer to her lips. The Saturday afternoon in early April was in the mid-seventies, which was perfect for being outdoors. And everyone in St. Louis knew that once spring came, it was baseball season. The older set who'd gotten creakier knees and larger bellies played slow-pitch softball instead.

Paige gestured to the cooler. "Sure you don't want one?"

"I'm good," Chandy replied. She'd agreed to attend Ahmed's softball game as part of her recent get-out-more plan. "As for my car, it's only been a few weeks. They said a minimum of a month."

Paige's husband came up to bat. "Come on, Ahmed! You can hit that ball!" Paige encouraged from her spot on the bleachers. Today was the first day of league play. "Well, cars do take time. At least you're driving a better rental."

"True. They keep changing them out. I must have scared the manager when I called to complain about the first car. Every time a better car becomes available, he calls me and swaps it with what I have. I don't know what I'll get next. A Hummer?"

"So how are you and Craig doing?" Paige asked, reaching for the bag of pretzels she'd brought. She poured Chandy a handful.

"I don't think things with Craig are going to work," Chandy said in between bites. "We went to a movie last night and, well…"

She paused and then spilled the truth. "We're running out of things to say. He's just too shy. And worse, he's already imagining us married and he wants me to meet his mother. I can't move that fast. I mean, I'm just not that into him."

Paige made a face. "Eek. What a shame. He's a nice guy."

"I didn't say he wasn't nice. Just that there's no spark."

"He's not sexy?" Paige asked.

Chandy hesitated. After all, Craig was Ahmed's good friend. "Um…"

Paige sipped her beer. "Hey, no worries. I'm agreeing with you here. Ahmed might think Craig walks on water but we're women. We need some spice, especially in the bedroom. I can't picture Craig in that department."

"Since he barely raises my temperature I don't want to," Chandy admitted.

"I don't need to hear any more. Craig's out. There are other fish in the sea."

"Yeah, but I'm not a very good fisherman."

"You're too funny." Paige scanned the crowd and then

poked Chandy. "Hey, what about him? I'd forgotten he played in this league. He's hot." Paige pointed.

"Who?"

"Didn't you get a chance to meet him? He's got your car." Paige stood and waved. "Hey, Justin. Over here."

Now Chandy saw him, and she resisted the impulse to hide as Justin McCall approached. He wore shorts and a T-shirt and carried a ball glove. Paige wasn't kidding. Justin's raw sex appeal had most women watching him as he walked by.

"You playing today?" Paige asked when he got within five feet.

"Our game's up next," Justin said. His eyes were hidden by his ball cap and sunglasses, but his full lips curved into a smile as he said, "Hi, Chandy."

She couldn't quite look at him. "Justin."

Paige stood, her attention momentarily diverted. Her subsequent shout of "That's it, honey! Way to steal that base!" gave Chandy a moment to compose herself. That was until Paige sat back down and patted the spot next to her. "Take a load off, Justin."

To Chandy's chagrin, he sat, putting Paige in the middle. "How's the Porsche handling?" he asked.

The Porsche 911 convertible was Ahmed's pride and joy. "Did you see it when you came in? Today's a perfect day to have the top down," Paige said. "Ahmed's thrilled. We recommended you to Chandy. That's why you have her car."

"And I thank you greatly for that." He leaned back against the bleachers.

As the inning changed, Chandy asked, "So where's Ben?"

"Concession stand. He'll be along in a minute. He ran into some friends. There he is now."

Ben came trudging up the bleachers, a boy his age at his side. "Hey, Chandy."

"Dr. McDaniel," Justin corrected his son.

"Chandy's fine," she insisted. "How are you, Ben?"

"Good. I'm pitching my first baseball game next week. You should come and watch."

Paige lowered her sunglasses and Chandy read the question in her friend's eyes.

"I treated Ben in the E.R. for a concussion a few weeks ago. That's when Justin and I first ran into each other. I told you about that. Remember?" Chandy said.

Paige had always been adept at putting two and two together and her mouth dropped open. She pointed at Chandy and then at Justin. "Oh. You and Justin."

"Went to high school together," Justin inserted smoothly, aware of teenage ears.

"Yes, we did," Chandy added, the warning in her tone clear. No need to add more than that, which hopefully would put an immediate end to Paige's earlier matchmaking ideas.

"Okay, got it," Paige replied. Chandy didn't appreciate the knowing smirk Paige gave her. Her friend leaned over. "You owe me this story," she whispered.

"There's nothing to tell," Chandy replied in the same hushed tone.

"Liar. You said in the E.R. he was an ex-boyfriend. You've been keeping stuff from me."

Chandy deliberately turned her attention back to the softball game.

Ahmed's team won, and everyone went down to the sidelines. Ahmed shook hands with Justin. "Hey, good to see you. I guess my team will play yours at some point."

"In a few weeks," Justin confirmed.

"Shame it wasn't today. Honey, everyone's headed to Chewie's for a celebratory drink. We need to go."

"Chandy, are you coming with us?" Paige asked.

Chandy shook her head, her ponytail swishing. "No. You two go ahead. I'll catch up with you another time."

Paige's eyebrows moved together, and then her face relaxed. "Well, if you're sure. I'll call you later. You and I have things to talk about." Paige gave her a brief wave as she left, cooler strap over her shoulder.

"So are you staying? Going to watch me play?" Justin asked. He'd moved closer, his six-two body less than eight inches away.

She glanced up and faltered. "No. Actually I'm leaving. I only came because Paige asked and…"

He lowered his sunglasses, his eyes full of obvious mirth. "Chicken?"

How many times had he called her that in high school? There was the time he'd dared her to cross the log over Benson's Creek. Then there was the time she'd snuck out of her house after dark. Or the time she'd done a triple off the high dive at the city pool. She was no chicken.

"Why would I be afraid to watch a softball game? I just saw one, didn't I?" Chandy asked, glad Ben was on a trip to the bathroom and couldn't hear the exchange.

Justin shrugged, serious now. "I was just wondering and making sure it wasn't me. You were pretty mad when you left my shop."

A dull ache settled in her chest. "We've said all there is to say."

He placed his hand on her forearm. "Fine. Then let's find new things to talk about. Stay and watch me play. I'll buy you a pizza afterward. Thin crust with hamburger, onions, pepperoni and no mushrooms."

He'd remembered her favorite toppings and crust, and despite herself she smiled. "You always were an irresistible charmer."

He grinned. "Yeah, that's me." His gaze held hers. "Did it work?"

He lifted his hand and she glanced at her watch, breaking the magnetic connection. "I can stay for a little while. But I won't take you up on that pizza."

"Maybe next time, then," he said. A small pleasurable tingle fired through her, and she nodded noncommittally.

"Hey, Justin. Stop flirting and get over here. We're warming up!" one of his teammates called.

"That's my cue." Justin jogged into the infield and soon Ben returned and plopped next to her, soda in one hand and cell phone in the other.

"I'm impressed you can text with one hand, but don't you ever put that down?" Chandy indicated his phone.

"Chad wanted to know what the algebra homework was. I finished mine, but he lost the assignment sheet. Only seven weeks to go and school is out."

"I guess summer is around the corner."

Ben nodded. "Dad makes me do my homework the moment I walk in the door, even on Fridays. I'm ready for a long break."

"Your dad sounds tough but wise. On weekends my grandpa allowed me to wait until Sunday to do my homework."

Ben set the soda down so he could text with both thumbs. "He worries too much about my grades. He wants me to go to college. I think it's because he never got to go. But I'll get there."

In her line of work, Chandy had discovered that teenagers spoke what was on their mind to any audience willing to listen. Ben was no different.

"So you feel a lot of pressure?"

"Sometimes. But it's everywhere. Even at school the guidance counselors push you to pick a career path. How do I know what I want to do for the rest of my life? I just want a date. Like with her." He pointed to an attractive college-aged female whose shorts and shirt clearly displayed her assets.

Chandy grinned. "Down, boy."

Ben didn't seem too upset. "Yeah, she's out of my league."

"She's far too old for you."

"I can still dream," Ben replied, and then he got

another text, which distracted him for a moment. Justin's team was much more evenly matched with its opponent than Ahmed's team had been, and the innings were taking longer. Justin was playing shortstop, and he caught the ball on a pop fly, ending the bottom of the third.

As he ran to the dugout he gave her a thumbs-up. She hadn't seen Justin play ball since the spring of her junior year of high school, when the Chenille Tigers varsity baseball team had gone all the way to the state play-offs.

The Tigers had placed second, the highest showing in school history. Her senior year the team hadn't even made it past the semifinals. Then again, Justin had been one of the star players and his move to Chicago had left a huge void.

"So do you like playing baseball?" Chandy asked Ben.

"Yep. I'm hoping that if I play well enough I'll get called up to JV or varsity before the season's out. That's my goal."

JV was junior varsity, the level in between freshman and varsity. "Did your dad play in Chicago? He was really good, you know. Did he ever tell you they were second in state?"

Ben didn't look up from typing his next text. "No, he didn't. I don't remember much about Chicago. But I know my dad didn't like it."

Chandy glanced over to where Justin stood in the dugout. Before Justin's dad died, Justin had spent hours in the batting cages working on his swing. Sports had been the only thing he'd loved as much as her. He'd given up both.

"I really need to get going," she told Ben.

He glanced up then. "You're not staying until the end?"

"No. Tell your dad I'm sorry and I'll talk to him soon."

"Hey, you could talk to him at my game. Are you going to come?"

She hesitated. "Um…"

"It's at 4:00 p.m. Thursday at Khoury Field. You can find it on Google Maps."

Thursday was her early day—she stopped seeing patients at noon. Normally she headed to the crisis nursery. "I can't guarantee I can come. But I'll try. If not, I'm sure you'll be awesome."

He took a drink of soda. "I hope so."

The drive home was uneventful and she'd been home for about two hours before her cell phone started ringing. She noted the number and answered. "Hey, Chase, what's up?"

"I wanted to give you the news myself," her brother said without preamble.

She gripped the phone tighter. Her grandfather was turning eighty-five at the end of May and she worried about him. Still, Chase's tone had been more excited than upset. "It's not bad, is it?"

"Heck no. Miranda and I are expecting again."

Excitement followed relief. "That's great!"

Her brother laughed. "Yeah. Thanks. It's twins. Who saw that coming? We certainly didn't."

"It's not like you don't know how these things happen," Chandy joked, sitting on her couch.

"No, but we thought one was all we'd get. Not two at once. Although we're thrilled."

"Of course you are and congratulations again. When is the lucky day?" She reached for the TV remote.

"Miranda's due November fifteenth, but the doctor says twins come early. Want to be a godmother?"

Excitement filled her and she put the remote down without turning on the set. "You know I do!"

"Then count on it. Hey, while I'm thinking of it, are you coming to Chenille for Easter?"

"Unless there's an emergency, I'll see you in two weeks." Chandy's phone began to beep, indicating she had another call. She glanced at it quickly. A number she didn't recognize. "That's my other line."

"Then I'll see you soon. I have to go call more people with the news, anyway. Love you!"

Chase hung up and Chandy switched over. "Hello?"

"Hi, Chandy, it's Justin."

Too nervous to sit still, she stood and went into the kitchen. "Hi. Did you win your game?" She grabbed a glass and filled it with water.

"Yeah, but that's not why I called. Ben told me he asked you to attend his baseball game."

She took a sip. "He did."

"He shouldn't have done that. You don't need to feel obligated to go. I told him he shouldn't have put you in an awkward position."

Chandy wasn't quite certain how to reply. While

Justin had just relieved her of disappointing Ben, she didn't like that'd he'd come down on his son because of her. "I told Ben I didn't know if I'd make it. I handled the situation fine by myself."

"I didn't want you to think I put him up to that."

"Justin, it's okay he asked me. That's what kids do. His first time as starting pitcher is a big moment. I'm sure he's inviting everyone."

"He did invite everyone at work. But you don't have to come if you don't want to."

"How about you let me make that decision? Unless you'd prefer that I stay away…"

Silence fell on the line. Then he said, "No, I'd like to see you. But this is uncharted territory for both of us."

She tried to make light of it. "Like I keep telling you, no biggie. Water under the bridge."

"Chandy. I know you're lying. We should talk."

He'd seen through her. Maybe he was right. Maybe she should listen to what he had to say. Chandy chewed on her lower lip. "Okay. We obviously know some of the same people. We could be crossing paths in the future."

"Exactly. And I would like the opportunity to apologize. Please."

"Fine. I'll talk to you at Ben's game—that is, if I attend. But please make sure he knows I wasn't offended by his request. It was okay to ask me. In his mind, we just went to high school together. That's a legitimate connection."

"I'll talk to him again," Justin promised.

She returned to the sofa. "Thank you."

"All right then."

They'd run out of things to say, and the awkward pause stretched. "If you show up, I'll see you at the game," Justin finished. "Bye."

Chandy ended the call and leaned back against the sofa. She turned on the TV, and she pressed the volume button. She had four days to make her decision.

THURSDAY AFTERNOON Chandy made her way to the bleachers on the home side of the ball field. After much internal debate and wrestling with her emotions, she'd decided she needed closure.

She knew she risked further hurt—after all, if things had gone as planned, she and Justin would have attended sporting events as husband and wife, full of pride at their little one's achievements. Instead, she was an interloper.

She reached up, making certain her dark sunglasses hid her eyes. She had to get out of the past, leave it behind. That was what today was all about, clearing the air. She'd come to the conclusion that if she let Justin apologize, maybe she could free herself and move forward.

"Glad you could make it," Justin said as she sat down beside him. "I hope you didn't have to rearrange your schedule."

"No. I don't see patients after twelve on Thursdays. So coming here didn't put me out."

His arms flexed as he reached into the cooler at his feet and grabbed a plastic bottle. "Water?"

"That'd be great. Thanks."

Their fingers connected as he handed her the bottle, sending a tingle of awareness up her arm. His eyes widened for a brief moment as if he felt the same thing, but then he turned his attention to the home players taking the field for practice. As he should, Chandy decided. Today was not about rekindling what they had.

Ben was on the mound, and he threw a few warm-up pitches before the umpire gestured to both coaches, and the team captains moved forward so they could get the game started.

"I haven't watched high school ball since our junior year," she ventured, uncomfortable with the silence.

Justin rotated his neck and arched an eyebrow. "Not even for your nephews?"

"My brother Chris's kids play in a league, but that's in Iowa. I get my fix by watching the Cardinals play. I became hooked when my grandfather visited St. Louis during my residency and rented a huge party room."

"Do you go home much?"

"I usually fly up on holidays, but I haven't gotten there as often as I'd like lately. I'm headed back for Easter, though."

"Well, hopefully Ben's team will win and make coming out here worthwhile."

"They're kids. Just remember, you weren't all that great when you first started."

He cocked his head, his expression dubious but eyes full of mirth. "Are you kidding? I was a stud. I rocked. You thought I was sexy."

"Please. I felt sorry for you," Chandy said, sipping her water.

"Yeah, right. Try to sell me another story." Justin laughed, and the sound seemed to transport her back in time to when all was well between them and teasing each other was second nature.

They watched as Ben and his teammates moved into their respective positions. The first batter approached the plate.

"Come on, Ben!" Justin yelled as Ben wound up for the first pitch. He delivered a strike.

"That's okay!" someone on the other side yelled.

"Way to go, Ben!" Justin called out. "Now two more." He turned to Chandy and revealed his crossed fingers. "The first batter you face in each game is so huge. It's even more important your first time on the mound."

Ben's next pitch went high, and the count was 1–1. He was outside with the next ball, and Chandy could see Ben's irritation in the way he kicked the dirt. She leaned forward, elbows on her knees, chin on her fingertips. The count became 3–2. Do-or-die time. The batter swung at the fastball that crossed the plate…and missed.

"Yes!" Chandy jumped up and clapped. "Good job, Ben."

Justin was on his feet, as well, and he impulsively gave her a hug. "His first strikeout!" Then, realizing he had Chandy pressed to his chest, Justin let her go.

Chandy simply smiled, trying to regain her self-control. That mere second in Justin's arms had been enough to create raw physical longing, a sensation she hadn't felt in fifteen years.

If Ben saw them, he didn't acknowledge them, but

he was grinning ear-to-ear as the home crowd cheered its approval. Not that the rest of the inning went easy for him. The next batter managed to get a base hit, as did the following, but a double play ended the drive and sent Ben's team up to bat.

"You're really into this," Justin remarked as the game went on.

"Baseball's my favorite sport. I bought in for season tickets to the Cardinals with a group of people. I get to see about ten games a year."

The inning ended with no score, as a lack of hits stranded Ben's teammates on their respective bases. Ben jogged back to the mound.

Chandy sipped her water as the game played on. She'd worn a short-sleeve sweater, but being out in the sun had heated her skin. Or maybe it was the very attractive guy sitting next to her, whose T-shirt-covered chest revealed that he was pretty darn fit. Her stomach had fluttered when he'd hugged her.

As part of her bachelor's degree she'd taken organic chemistry. So she could say with certainty that Justin was simply a walking pheromone where she was concerned—and always had been.

The game intensified, and they didn't have much chance to talk about anything. She realized that a baseball game probably wasn't the best venue for what needed to be said anyway.

She was also enjoying herself too much to spoil the afternoon. By the top of the seventh, Ben's team was up by two with the overall score 8–6. High school games only went seven innings, if Ben held on to the lead his team would win.

She could tell he was getting tired, but unlike the pros, freshman teams didn't have a bull pen. Ben's team had a tournament this weekend, and Saturday's starting pitcher was currently playing right field.

Ben walked the first batter.

"That's okay, Ben!" Chandy shouted. A few other mothers of Ben's teammates chimed in, echoing her encouragement.

"This is the part where I get nervous," Justin admitted. "The last game they played they blew the lead and lost by five."

"Hush. Don't be bad luck," Chandy chided, amazed that she and Justin had relaxed during the game. "You can get the next guy!" she called to Ben.

But Ben's slider didn't work, and the next player hit a pop fly to right. The fielder caught it, but the opposing team advanced to second. Ben faltered on the next guy, and before too long, the count was one out and bases loaded. Worse, only one run was needed to tie the game, and that runner waited at third.

"Luckily I'm not the type to bite my fingernails or they'd be nubs," Justin remarked. "I just want him to win the first time out, you know? This is one of those life-changing moments. If he wins, it's going to boost his confidence tenfold."

Chandy understood. It was like her first figure-skating competition. She'd placed seventh, crushing her ambitions. After one other competition, she'd realized she wasn't cut out to be an Olympian and had moved on to something else.

"He's doing fine. He's pitching to the bottom of their lineup. He'll get the next guy," Chandy soothed.

"He has to get the next guy," Justin said. "A home run or even a base hit will doom their chances. They need to close this out."

Chandy reached out and put a reassuring hand on his arm. "It'll be fine. Stop worrying."

"You don't understand. He's not your son."

She yanked her hand away as if he'd slapped it. "No, you're right. He's not."

JUSTIN KNEW HE'D MESSED UP the moment he saw the stricken expression cross Chandy's face. Hell, he'd been so worried about Ben, when really he shouldn't be. Ben was just happy to be out there playing. The pressure was all on Justin's side.

Justin cursed under his breath, and added a second curse to the first as she slid her sunglasses back on. "Damn it. Chandy, I'm sorry."

She held up her palm. "Just stop. It's not that big of a deal."

But it was. He knew she'd figured out the timeline of Ben's age. And seconds ago he'd tossed that fact in her face. He wanted to talk to her about it, but Ben's arm was in motion, distracting him. The ball sailed across the plate—a strike. Ben needed two more of those. The crowd of parents and students rose to their feet, everyone still and silent. Two consecutive strikes later, another batter gone.

"One more out," Justin breathed, determined to talk to Chandy after the game. He would somehow restart the fun they'd been having, the comfortable companionship that, until he'd screwed up, had been the first chink in Chandy's armor.

Now his son's crucial moment came first. "Come on, Ben! You can do it!"

Ben's head moved as he nodded to the catcher, and then he straightened, went in for the windup, and delivered. The batter connected and popped the ball deep into left.

"Catch it, Tony!" some mother screamed.

Out in left field Ben's teammate had his glove up. Everyone seemed to freeze as the ball dropped, and then there were excited shrieks and cheers of joy as Tony extended his arm. Game over. Ben's team had won.

The home team fans were jubilant, and giving high fives, while on the field the teams lined up to shake hands and say "good game" over and over. Parents complimented Justin on Ben's pitching and another parent suggested the team go out for ice cream to celebrate their first win.

Justin gripped both of Ben's shoulders and gave him a congratulatory shake and then a fist bump. "You did it!"

Ben couldn't stop smiling; clearly he was in the best kind of daze. "Thanks for coming," he said when he finally noticed Chandy, and then some girl raced up to hug him, capturing his interest.

"I appreciate you being here," Justin told her. "How about joining us for ice cream and then you and I can find a quiet corner? I've been a real cad, especially with what I said earlier."

But at that moment her phone began to ring, and much to Justin's dismay she took the device out of her purse, glanced at the number and held up a finger, indicating he wait. "Chandy McDaniel."

The crowd remained thick as people milled about and confirmed plans to meet at the local ice cream shop. "Dad, you coming?" Ben called.

"Yeah. Hold up, though. Chandy's on the phone."

As Ben wandered off to tell his friends, Chandy finished her call. "Everything okay?" Justin asked.

She shook her head, her blond hair swishing against the tops of her shoulders. "No. I have to go to the crisis nursery. Normally I'm there on Thursdays and it's an emergency. They need me."

Disappointment washed over Justin, but he admired Chandy's commitment to such a worthy cause. Despite his deepest wish, he knew he didn't have the right to ask her to stay. "Some other time then," he said.

"Perhaps," Chandy said, and Justin could tell she'd already retreated into that place inside herself, brought back down the professional wall that he'd seen in the E.R.

Ben returned. "You coming?" he asked Chandy.

She smiled at Ben, a smile Justin wished she'd bestow on him, as well. "No, I can't. But it was a great game. You were awesome."

"Thanks. Sorry you can't come with us," Ben said.

Then, as the girl who'd hugged him yelled, "Ben, you coming?" he turned away to answer.

However, as Justin watched Chandy walk toward her rental, a Cadillac Escalade, he realized he couldn't let go so easily. Not this time.

He had things to say to her, and baseball hadn't been the ideal place. They would need to be alone.

He wanted to be able to peel back the layers that protected her. Chandy had always been so full of life and now there was darkness where the light had been.

He had to make things right. And, as that brief hug in the bleachers had shown, he was still attracted to her. The grown woman was even more intriguing than Chandy had been as a teenager. Maybe they could start over. It was worth a try, wasn't it?

Damn it, he suddenly wanted a second chance.

Chapter Four

"So that's the whole story," Chandy finished. She reached for her glass of white wine. Luckily she wasn't driving or working tomorrow. It had taken two glasses of liquid courage to reveal almost everything from her past to Paige.

Her friend wiped at her eyes and leaned back against the dining room chair. "I never would have guessed. You've been through so much."

"Tell me about it," Chandy said, rising to clear the last of the dinner dishes. Ahmed was on a guys-only fly-fishing trip, so Chandy had invited Paige over for dinner and a movie. She hadn't meant to confess all the secrets of her soul, but once Paige asked about Justin, the wine had started flowing and so had Chandy's story.

"So where do you two go from here?" Paige asked.

"I don't know." Chandy returned from the kitchen with two glasses of water and a bowl full of chocolate-covered strawberries, Chandy's favorite indulgence.

"I think you need to tell him. You need to clear the air," Paige declared before she took a bite of fruit.

"And how do I do that? Do I just blurt out that I

miscarried our child? What does it matter now? What's done is done."

"We've only been friends for a few years, and I hope you still consider me a good one after what I'm going to say. He should be sharing this burden with you. Once you unload it, I think you'll be able to finally move on."

"But what does ruining his life do? I thought of that after I left the baseball game. It just puts one more person in misery. It's not like we're going to be dating."

"Why not? Would you like to date him again?" Paige asked.

"No. We're over," Chandy replied, a little too quickly.

Paige let the lie slide as she fingered the stem of her wineglass. "Did I ever tell you I'm a breast cancer survivor?"

"You? But you're only..."

"Forty," Paige filled in. "I've been cancer-free for six years now. I'm one of the younger ones diagnosed with the disease. I learned I had it one year after Ahmed and I were married. At first I didn't want to tell him. My greatest fear wasn't the cancer, but rather that Ahmed would no longer find me attractive. They told me I'd lose my hair and that I was going to lose my breasts."

Paige glanced down. "These are replacements."

"I never would have guessed," Chandy said.

"These new breasts meant I lived," Paige said. "And as for Ahmed, I couldn't bear telling him. Yet a few days after the doctor's diagnosis, I finally got up the courage. I don't know why I doubted his feelings—for the news didn't drive him away. He stood by me and put up with my massive mood swings all during the chemo. He loved me despite my scars. He was my hero. I can't imagine having gone through it alone."

"He's a great guy."

"So is Justin. Ahmed and I don't hang out with him outside of softball, but I've seen him enough times to know. Besides, I'm a great judge of character, and Ahmed's even better. Justin will surprise you when you tell him, and then maybe you'll find some peace. So listen to what he has to say. You won't know what the future holds until you both clear the air."

Chandy leaned back against the chair with a thump. "It's obvious you're married to a psychiatrist."

Paige grinned. "Yeah, well, what can I say? Some of the mumbo jumbo rubs off, and Ahmed's one of the best. Trust me on this, though. I know what I'm talking about."

"I'll think about it," Chandy promised. But once Monday arrived, she promptly pushed Justin and contacting him out of her mind, despite the three messages he'd left on her cell phone.

Not that ignoring him worked. He haunted two of her dreams. She found herself wondering how life might have turned out differently, and she considered Paige's suggestion that maybe she just needed to blurt it out.

Yet there were Easter preparations to make, and Chandy, not normally the procrastinator, delayed calling Justin back. And then, it was the holiday weekend, and she went home to Chenille Thursday night so she could see her family. She flew in on the McDaniel

Manufacturing company jet, and waiting on the tarmac to greet her was her brother Chase.

"Hey!" he called, and the moment she stepped onto the pavement he enveloped her in a big hug. "It's good to see you."

He caught her up on town gossip as he drove to their grandfather's estate. Even though the six-bedroom house on two acres was far too large for just one person, Leroy refused to downsize.

As soon as she left the car, her brother Chris, his wife, Joan, and their two sons, Cory and Clayton, gave her huge hugs. Her sister, Cecilia, was also present with husband, Jesse, and daughter, Lanie. Since everyone except for Chase and Miranda lived outside Chenille, all were staying with Leroy until Easter Monday.

Dinner was energetic and boisterous, and as tradition dictated, followed by family game night. By 9:00 p.m. things began to wind down. Her grandfather was in jovial spirits, although it concerned Chandy how old he was looking. He'd lost weight and gained more wrinkles. But his spirit was strong, and she relaxed after Chase told her Leroy's last checkup had been fine. All was well.

"So is the parade tomorrow morning?" she asked. Forty years ago, deciding everyone needed to be off for Good Friday, Leroy had closed the plant for the day and started the annual parade.

"Of course. Wouldn't miss a year," Leroy said. "Miranda's in charge."

"She's really changed things up," Chase said.

"You're too kind. It was nothing." Sitting next to her

husband, Miranda squeezed Chase's hand. Already her belly rounded outward. Chandy smiled, but the moment was slightly bittersweet. The love between Chase and his wife was obvious, although they'd had a rocky start.

"Will your sister be joining us?" Chandy asked her.

"Not this year. She'll come in for Leroy's birthday party, though."

Every year over Memorial Day weekend, the entire family and tons of guests descended on the McDaniel lake house on Lone Pine Lake, about three hours north in Minnesota.

Leroy yawned, indicating it was time for bed. Chandy's childhood room was essentially the same as when she'd been a teenager. She'd taken some mementoes with her, but mostly she'd left things as they were, figuring she'd get all her stuff when she was permanently settled. Even now, she considered her condo a temporary place. Maybe someday she'd get married and…well, then she'd worry about her things. Until that time, her stuff was safe in Chenille.

She sat down at her vanity and opened the right top drawer. A gift for her fourteenth birthday, the vanity had everything a teenage girl could want, including a false-bottomed drawer.

In a fit of adolescent rage after losing the baby, she'd shredded all of the little reminders she'd kept of Justin. That was, all but the ones in this drawer. As she removed the first note, she could see where her tears had smeared the black ink. She unfolded the paper, the first note

Justin had ever given her, back in eighth grade. "Hey McDaniel. I think I like you. McCall."

Her lips curled upward; a nostalgic smile crept across her face. He'd tossed the folded note onto her desk, and then he'd turned around and ignored her the rest of the period.

She'd stared at his back the entire class, memorizing the patterns and texture of the red, black and tan long-sleeved flannel shirt he wore. After the bell he'd stood up, winked and asked her out. She'd had every intention of saying no. After all, he'd thrown a note at her saying he thought he liked her.

But the moment he'd hit her with those baby blues her stomach had fluttered and the denial had died. She'd said yes.

The rest was history. She folded the note, placing the age-stiffened paper back in the drawer. She turned over a photo—their first high school dance, homecoming, freshman year. She'd worn the latest fashion, which by today's standards would be described as a hideous, poofy lavender dress deserving to be burned. She'd loved it, though, and next to her Justin wore a white tux and matching lavender cummerbund.

That night had been their first adult kiss. Up until then all the kisses they'd shared had been sweet and chaste. The deep kiss had filled her with longing, yet he never pressured her for sex. She'd liked that about him. He respected her. Others her age had interesting sex stories, but then such was life in a small town where some boys and girls grew up too fast and had bad reputations far too early. Both Chandy and Justin had wanted more.

Chandy continued digging through the drawer, fingering a movie ticket for *Ghost,* a menu from their one-year-anniversary dinner and a Valentine's Day card.

Finally she opened the small box, the one he'd pressed into her hand the very last time she'd seen him. Inside, on a gold chain, two hearts were intertwined. The enclosed note said he'd love her forever.

A tear fell, and Chandy let the droplet flow. Then she angrily brushed it away and closed the box. She'd never forget and she'd always grieve for her baby, and all the others she'd never have. In reality she purposely hadn't moved on. She owed Justin the truth.

Perhaps it was finally time. If she told Justin the truth, then perhaps she would stop blaming him as one of her therapists had maintained she was doing.

Chandy returned the false bottom and closed the drawer. She'd talk to Justin as soon as she got back.

THE CHENILLE EASTER PARADE started at 10:00 a.m., and by 9:45, spectators lined the streets. An hour later, Chandy left the McDaniel Manufacturing VIP booth. Everyone in her family was heading to lunch at Maxine's, the local restaurant on Main Street, for the fish special.

As they stopped to say hello to friends and colleagues, the family group easily got separated in the large crowd. Yet Chandy knew they'd all catch up at their table. So she took her time, stopping to talk to a former high school friend who was now an English teacher at Chenille High School. She'd made it another ten feet when she heard a male voice call, "Chandy? I mean, Dr. McDaniel?"

She turned to see Ben standing there, a big grin on his face. Next to him was his grandmother, who seemed slightly uncomfortable. "Hi, Chandy," Eleanor McCall said.

"Hi," Chandy managed, staring at Justin's mother. She'd changed, but then it had been fifteen years since that fateful day Eleanor McCall had driven away with her sons. Her hair was now gray and fell to her shoulders. She smiled awkwardly, her face covered with wrinkles caused by time and stress.

"What are you both doing here? I mean, I know the parade attracts visitors from all over, but..." Chandy shut her mouth, aware she was babbling. Still, they were two of the last people she would have expected to see. Chandy glanced around for Justin, but he was nowhere in sight.

"I moved back last October after I retired. Ben and Justin are here visiting me for Easter."

"Yeah, my dad's gone fishing with some high school friends. I said I'd take Grandma to the parade when she told me it was tradition."

"And a great escort you've been," Mrs. McCall said, beaming at her grandson with pride.

"Yeah, it wasn't that lame. A lot cooler than I thought it would be," Ben replied.

"Well, tell your dad I said hello. I'm late meeting my family for lunch. It's good seeing you, Ben. Mrs. McCall." And with that, Chandy tightened the belt of her pink spring trench coat and fled. As she made her way down the sidewalk, she could hear Ben explaining to his grandmother how Chandy had attended one of his games.

She arrived at Maxine's, stashed her coat and sat down at the table next to Chase. He leaned over. "You're pale. Are you okay?"

"I'm fine. Just ran into some people. A little surprised by the size of the crowd and out of breath trying to get here, that's all."

"Yeah, it gets crazier every year. The chamber of commerce loves it. The parade and tomorrow's egg hunt have actually become quite the tourist attractions. The hotel even fills up."

Lunch was a two-hour affair, and by the time everyone made it back to Leroy's, Chandy wanted a nap she was so stuffed. She changed into comfortable sweats, and had just crawled under her covers when her cell phone rang. She grabbed the phone, saw the name and groaned. Justin. She debated for only a second about sending the call to voice mail. "Hi, Justin."

"Hey. Heard you ran into my mom and Ben today." His deep voice came clearly through the line.

"I did. It was quite the surprise. I didn't know you were going to be in town."

She glanced around her room and experienced a sense of déjà vu, which doubled when he said, "Can you escape?"

She clutched the phone tighter as the same type of anticipatory flutters she'd experienced as a teenager sent giddy little chills tingling over her skin. How many times had he called her late at night the summer before their senior year and asked her that? And how many times had she snuck out to meet him?

She tried to stay calm. "I was about to take a nap."

"It's too beautiful a day to sleep. Meet me at the city park. The gazebo. That's nice and public."

He hadn't asked her to meet him on South Post Road, which ran alongside the edge of McDaniel Manufacturing. They'd spent many nights parked beneath the faint glow of the plant lights, although, until that very last night on Old Quarry Road, they'd only indulged in heavy kissing.

He must have sensed her hesitation, for he added, "Please, Chandy. My mom's serving dinner at six so there's a time limit. Come on, let's talk. Don't we owe ourselves that?"

Chandy closed her eyes. Even if she said no, she was now too keyed up to get any rest. "Okay. I'll be there in twenty minutes." And then, before she changed her mind, she hung up.

JUSTIN PACED THE WORN, gray wood floor of the city park gazebo. The white, octagon-shaped structure was about fifteen feet wide. During festivals, orchestra members would sit on metal folding chairs and play for a huge crowd, but today it was empty. They could move to a nearby picnic table if they wanted to sit.

He'd arrived early, leaving almost ten minutes after he'd called. He simply couldn't remain in his mother's small house any longer. Last October, when his mom had moved back to Chenille, he'd wondered if he'd see Chandy. But then he'd learned she'd moved away.

Today, knowing she'd be at the parade, he'd tried to hide out by going fishing with friends. He hadn't wanted to ruin the day for her. But since his mother and son had run into her, he knew he had to call.

He watched the parking lot, but instead of seeing a car arrive, he saw Chandy walking down the sidewalk, traveling on foot since Leroy's estate was about three quarters of a mile away. Justin left the gazebo and went to meet her.

"I needed the exercise," she said in greeting. "I devoured far too much of Maxine's fish special at lunch."

They began to stroll on the path around the lake. Justin couldn't stop looking at Chandy. She wore a blue tracksuit and had pulled her hair back into a ponytail. She looked so cute and casual that he had the sudden urge to kiss her. Instead he pointed to a set of picnic tables. He climbed onto one, and she sat on the edge of the other, a few feet away.

"Your mom looked well," Chandy said, breaking the silence.

"Yeah, she's finally happy."

"I didn't know she had come back."

"Since Derek and I left Chicago, there was no reason for her to stay. She still has a lot of friends in Chenille. They scrapbook, play bunco and stuff. She likes it here."

"I'm glad she's happy, but you could have warned me."

"I didn't think you'd run into her. I'm sorry. I should

have told you Ben and I were coming up. But after the way we left things at the game, I didn't want to seem like I was harassing you or following you when you didn't return my calls."

"I suppose that makes sense. Is Derek here?"

"No. He lives in Hawaii. He works with disadvantaged youth and was on call this weekend. He's also dating someone, and well, he probably won't visit until Christmas. But my mom is headed to Hawaii for Memorial Day."

"Sounds like he's really turned himself around."

"He has. It was about time."

"Just so you know, I told Paige about us. Our past, I mean."

Her abrupt change of subject surprised him. "Everything?"

"She's my friend and I needed to tell someone. I hope that doesn't make things awkward for you and Ahmed."

He mulled that over. "No, it's okay. I work on Ahmed's cars and we play in the same softball league. We're not confidants."

"Good, because I needed advice. Paige thought it might be good for me to hear you out. Clear the air."

"Which is what I've been saying all along."

Chandy nodded. "I know. I realize that but until now I wasn't ready to listen. I've been carrying around a lot of hurt, probably more so than I should. And that's a long time. Sadly it's become a part of me. I should be over what happened after you moved, but for some reason,

I'm not. It's like a scar. It fades, but it never goes away. You made me promises and you broke them."

"I'm so sorry." He pushed himself off the table and went to stand by her. She didn't shy away, which was a good sign. "I can't tell you how many times I started to call, how many letters I wrote. I thought it would be easy for you. Johnny Sims was in love with you for years. He was just waiting for me to get out of the way. I heard you went to prom with him."

"Because my grandfather said I had to keep up appearances after…" She paused, and her hands shook. "I didn't want Johnny. I wanted you. And you broke my heart."

Her words were like a knife through his heart.

"I hurt you. I realize that. I can't apologize enough. All I can do is try to explain. As the months went on I simply couldn't go back. I was a different person. A stupid idiot, yes, but one who thought he'd burned a bridge. I couldn't come back, especially not after failing to write or call."

"I waited for you. I went through hell. I just wanted to know you were okay."

Her lower lip trembled, and impulsively Justin reached out to gently caress her cheek. Her eyes widened at the contact.

"I'm so sorry," he repeated, his voice fiercer. "I can't tell you how much I hate myself. You're the last person I ever wanted to hurt. When I said I loved you, I meant it. But my life fell apart. I worked in a grocery store instead of playing ball. My grades tanked. I wasn't going to college. I wasn't worthy of you. Hell, maybe I never was."

WITH THOSE WORDS, CHANDY moved her head, breaking the contact. "You should have let me decide that."

He stood there, and her eyes welled with tears. "Instead you replaced me."

"Not intentionally." He paused, raked a hand through his hair. "No, I admit, that's a lie. Maybe I did. When I knew I could never come back here and be the man you deserved, I self-destructed. Not as bad as Derek, but close enough in my own way. My relationship with Ben's mother started as a one-night stand. She was two years older and I thought she was hot. She was my alcohol. For a while her attention numbed my pain. Made me forget what I couldn't have.

"We only got married because she was pregnant, but neither of us really wanted the other. When Ben came along life was tough, and eventually she bailed, wanting something more, something better."

He paced slightly. "Having Ben forced me to get my act together. I can't expect you to understand. It all sounds so lame, and I have no good excuses for hurting you."

Chandy fought back tears, wiping them away with her jacket cuff. "I feel so terrible," he told her. "Chandy, I'm so sorry. They're just words, I know, and I'll never be able to say them enough."

"No, it's fine. I understand but..."

She faltered, for really, what was there to say? Part of her wanted to hit him. Part of her wanted to scream. Part of her simply wanted to cry. But none of that would change what happened.

"I'm an ass," he concluded for her.

She shook her head, wanting to ease his pain despite her own. "We were just kids. We were young, naive and stupid."

"And I grew up the moment we drove out of here. A part of me died that day."

Her face contorted at those words, her tears replaced by anger. "A part of you died? What about me? Do you know what I went through?"

"No. I don't. And for whatever it was, I'm sorry. I had no right."

"No. You didn't." Her voice rose. "You made decisions that were not yours alone to make. You played God. You never thought I might need you. You were selfish. One word. All I needed was one word. Just one."

"I'm sorry."

"Stop saying that," she snapped. "Your apology is useless. It doesn't change what happened. I was pregnant. I needed you and you wouldn't even return my letters!"

"Pregnant?" Her announcement stunned him and he stepped backward. His mouth dropped open and eyes widened.

"Pregnant," she repeated, not relishing his shock. "I wanted to tell you. I told my grandfather you'd come home. That you'd never leave me, not intentionally. But you never called. Not one word! He said not to bother you, that we'd handle it, just the McDaniels. And then I miscarried and there was no point."

Now that she'd reached the end of her speech, angry tears ran down her cheeks in rivulets. She wiped them away, her nose congested and her chest heaving. "Not one word," she whispered. "All I needed was one word."

"Oh, God, Chandy. I…"

She held up her hand. "No. Don't apologize again. I thought that telling you might clear the air, make things better. I was wrong. It will never be all right."

She stopped, and he followed her gaze toward the parking lot. A brand-new black Corvette was cruising by the park. They could see the driver clearly. Chase. "What is he doing here?" Justin asked.

"Playing big brother like he's done so many times before. Yet maybe this time it's a good thing. I don't want to talk anymore today."

Chandy hopped off the picnic table and away from Justin. "I'd better go. We can finish this some other time. That is, if there's really anything left to say."

JUSTIN WATCHED AS SHE crossed the grass and climbed into the car. A moment later it roared away.

He began to walk toward his SUV. He'd never felt so low. He'd had the woman of his dreams, and he'd destroyed her life. He'd been stupid at seventeen. He'd thought he was being noble. Instead he'd been a jerk.

She'd lost their baby. Their child.

Chapter Five

"You didn't have to come rescue me," Chandy said the moment she slid into the passenger seat. The seat belt locked with a decisive click. "I'm a big girl now."

"We were all worried when you took off on a walk. You didn't tell anyone where you were going. And I certainly wasn't expecting you'd go meet Justin McCall. You okay?"

"Yeah, well..." Chandy turned her face and gazed out the window. "We just happened to run into each other."

"If you say so. The gossip that you both were here reached Leroy less than five minutes after you arrived. Mrs. Sussmann saw you."

"Old busybody," Chandy declared. Then she fell silent again, until they turned into the drive. "I told him about the baby."

Chase glanced at her as he parked. Looking concerned, he reached out and wiped away a traitorous tear that was running down her cheek. "Do you think that's wise?"

"I don't know." She opened the car door and stepped

out. She faced him over the expanse of black paint. "Time will tell."

"You have to try to let go of the past."

"That's what I'm doing so just drop it." She closed the door. "How do you get a car seat in there?"

Chase's grin was wicked. "I don't. This car is my one vice. Don't spoil it."

"But it doesn't carry a bike." Her brother loved to cycle and still competed in the occasional race.

"I still have my SUV. And yes, there's a car seat in the back. Permanently installed."

Chandy laughed, and then sobered. She gave Chase a small sad smile. "It's hard, you know. A car seat in the back was all I ever really wanted."

Chase came around and wrapped her in a big bear hug. "You're going to be okay, Chandy."

"I hope so."

"You will. Sorry to turn you in, but the inquisitor waits. He's worried about you."

Chase meant her grandfather, who told her to close the door after she entered his home office. Leroy clicked the computer mouse, sending the screen to sleep. Then he pressed a button on his iPod. "Found a new song and was downloading it," he told her, settling back into his burgundy leather chair.

That had Chandy smiling. Even at eighty-five, her grandfather showed no signs of slowing down. He was a little kid when it came to the latest technology. He absorbed things like a sponge and knew how to use every application on his smartphone.

He swung around and placed both of his arms on his

desk and pinned her with his gaze. "I heard Justin's in town. How are you handling that?"

Her grandfather also always got straight to the point, which was sometimes an uncomfortable experience. She squirmed. "Is that why you sent Chase out looking for me? There's nothing to worry about. I'm not seventeen anymore."

Leroy sighed. "He's caused you a lot of pain. Do you really want to give him another chance?"

Chandy gripped the edge of the chair and chose her words carefully. "He's got my car. It's at his shop being repaired. We've discovered we know a lot of the same people…"

Leroy jumped in quickly. "I don't want you hurt."

"I can take care of myself. I'm not a child any longer and he and I should discuss what happened."

"I'm not so sure."

"Well, it's my decision. I can run my own life and have been doing a pretty good job of it lately, wouldn't you say?"

"You have, which is why I'm worried. The last thing I want for you is a setback. Do you know how helpless I felt when you lost the baby? I couldn't do anything to protect you. You were mine to protect, Chandy, and I failed to keep you and your child safe. I don't trust him not to hurt you again."

Against the dark leather, Leroy's hair seemed even whiter than it had the last time she'd come to visit. He also looked as if he'd shrunk. She remembered all those times when he'd sat in his chair, so large and powerful. When she'd been a child, he'd seemed huge. Almost bigger than life. Now he was smaller. Older. A bit less forceful and scary. But as he smiled she could see the love in his eyes—the affection he had for her.

"I admit I'm afraid, but I believe this is fate's way of finally letting me have some peace. I've carried enough hurt and pain around. I need to let it go. Justin and I made and lost a child. He has the right to know that."

"No." Leroy's voice was sharp, and she stiffened.

"It's too late. I told him today," she said.

Her grandfather's eyes narrowed. "Why open that wound again?"

"It was already open. It never closed, not for me. And seeing him again was like ripping the scab off. It hurt and I cried, but I want to heal this time. I want to finally be free."

"Your entire life is still in front of you. Trust me on this. Leave this thing with Justin alone."

She rose to her feet. "I don't know if I can."

Leroy smiled sadly. "I only want what's best for you," he told her. "And Justin isn't it."

"You may be right, but this is a decision I have to make for myself." Chandy bent over to give her grandfather a kiss on the cheek and left the room.

The next morning dawned bright and beautiful, in direct contrast to the melancholy Chandy felt. While she'd had a great time Friday evening with her family, her thoughts kept coming back to Justin and the bomb she'd dropped on him. She'd reached for her cell phone several times to call him, but something had always stopped her fingers from dialing.

Worse, she'd had a restless night's sleep, and even

though it was almost 10:00 a.m., she felt as if she could go back to bed and sleep for hours. But family duty called, and once again she was on hand for one of Chenille's annual traditions.

Unlike many who were dressed in more casual attire, like jeans, the McDaniels always dressed up for the town's annual Easter egg hunt. So Chandy wore a light spring floral dress, a big floppy white hat and pink leather ballet flats.

The Chenille Chamber of Commerce billed the hunt as one of the largest in the Midwest. Fifteen thousand eggs was a huge number, and the entire hillside of the city park was covered with blue, pink, yellow, green and purple plastic ovals as far as the eye could see. At the crack of dawn, city workers, using a tractor-pulled seeder modified for the purpose, had spread them everywhere.

"It always looks so wonderful," Chase's wife, Miranda, said. She'd dressed in a bright yellow maternity dress with matching hat, and her belly rounded outward. Her three-year-old son, Bobby, clung to her hand, wearing blue madras shorts and a white collared shirt and carrying his Easter basket. He was positively adorable.

"When, Mommy? When do we get to start?" Bobby asked, his face upturned.

"Soon, honey," Miranda said.

All around, children and parents began to gather, waiting for the official whistle to blow and for the ribbon to drop. When that happened, all the children would swarm the hillside, scooping up as many eggs as possible. Every egg would disappear in less than half an hour.

"Chandy!" Hearing her name, Chandy turned to see a former high school classmate. Chandy and Abby had lost touch their junior year when Abby and her family had moved to Des Moines. Next to Abby was a toddler, and in her arms she held a child about five months old.

"Hey, Abby. How are you?"

"Great. I didn't know you lived in Chenille."

Chandy shook her head. "I don't. I'm just here for the holiday, visiting my family. You, too?"

"No. Richard and I moved back last month. I took a job in product development at McDaniel so we relocated. Richard's in sales. He can work from anywhere as long as he has an Internet connection."

Her son tugged her hand and Abby called to her husband, "Hey, Richard. Come take Joey."

Her husband, also a member of Chandy's graduating class, headed over. He took his son's hand, relieving his wife of the job of watching him. "Hey, Chandy. How are you?"

"Great, thanks." She stood there a tad awkwardly. Richard and Abby had dated in high school, but they hadn't been as serious as Chandy and Justin. Yet obviously they'd worked out the details somehow, for here they were, married with kids.

"So what's new with you?" Abby asked.

"Not much." Chandy briefly filled Abby in on her life in St. Louis and offered to add her to her Facebook friend list.

Abby switched her daughter to the other arm.

"Richard's on Facebook and I probably should be, but being a mom of two keeps me far too busy. That's why I took this new job. It allows me to stay home more."

The whistle sounded, and kids screamed and took off, parents racing after them. Richard and Joey were in the mix. "Oh, darn. I thought I had more time. I need to get out my camera and follow them."

Abby began to dig into the diaper bag. "Here, will you hold Clarissa?"

Abby thrust the baby forward and Chandy grabbed her. Chandy cradled the baby and big brown eyes widened as Clarissa stared, her mouth hidden by a pacifier. Her face was surrounded by the ruffles of a sunbonnet that perfectly matched her dress. Chandy had the worst case of baby longing. "You are such a cute thing," she cooed at Clarissa.

"She is a cutie," Justin agreed, his voice flowing over Chandy like warm chocolate. She turned. He stopped next to them, and Chandy couldn't help noticing how handsome he looked in his chinos and a polo shirt.

Abby had retrieved her camera and she reached for her daughter. "Wow, Justin. Good to see you. You look great. I didn't know you and Chandy were still a couple."

"We aren't," Chandy said quickly, her arms achingly aware that they were empty of soft, sweet baby.

Abby appeared flustered. "Oh, I'm sorry. I just assumed. You were so close in high school. Anyway, I've got to get out there..." She backed away several steps, eager to escape to her husband and son. "Good seeing you both. I really should help Richard."

"We'll catch up later," Chandy said, knowing they probably wouldn't. Abby disappeared down the hill.

"Sorry about that," Justin said with a wry smile.

"It's no big deal." Chandy began to walk away, toward where children were scooping up eggs as fast as they could put them into their pastel baskets. She had family out there. But she didn't have her own child. She'd always be just on the edges…the outsider looking in.

Justin caught up with her, reached out and grabbed her arm. He whirled her around. "Hey, stop. Come talk to me. What's wrong? Is it what happened between us yesterday?"

She bit her lower lip, but it was too late. He'd already seen the tears in her eyes that she'd tried to hide. He cursed. "Damn it. I didn't mean to make you cry. Hell. I keep upsetting you."

"Just leave me alone."

"I can't. Besides, you don't want to go out there like this."

He was right. Chandy McDaniel crying at the Easter egg hunt would be prime gossip for the likes of Mrs. Sussmann and her cronies, and her brother the CEO and her grandfather didn't need that kind of embarrassment.

"Follow me," Justin said. He tossed an arm over her shoulder and Chandy let him lead her away. Leaving with Justin would be gossip, too, but at least not the damaging kind.

And she did want to leave. The children's laughter, normally music to her ears, was instead inducing pain.

She was hypersensitive lately, ever since Justin had come back into her life.

Today, watching all the parents with their happy kids, the truth had hit her like the blow of an atom bomb. She wanted what they had. She was missing something vital from her life. No matter how many times she told herself she was okay being single, or that she was all right with never having her own child, she wasn't.

She and Justin headed toward the table where they'd sat the previous day. They were far enough away from the crowd not to be noticed or overheard. "Want to tell me about it?"

"Not really," she replied. What good would making Justin's life miserable do? She didn't want vengeance. She wanted peace. And peace didn't come from hurting people.

"Tell me how I can fix this."

There was no way to fix what was irrevocably broken.

"I seem to be constantly making you unhappy, which is the last thing I want to do."

"I know." Chandy sat on the bench, and while Justin sat next to her, he left three feet of space between them. She wiped the last of her tears with her dress sleeve, leaving small wet smudges a few inches below her shoulder.

"Do you ever wish things could have worked out differently?" she asked.

"All the time. Even more so since that day in the E.R. I screwed up. Saying I was seventeen doesn't give me an excuse. I hurt you. You lost our child. I'll forever pay for that."

He sounded as if he'd had a hard time lately wrestling with his own demons.

"So does life ever get easier? Does the guilt ever go away?" she asked.

"Hell no." Justin shook his head vehemently and gave a bitter laugh. "I wish it did. Do you know that I haven't dated anyone in years? Not because I like being alone, but because Ben will learn how to treat women from my example. I don't want him having casual affairs. I don't want him hurting anyone. And trust me, no one ever compared to you."

"Wow." Chandy absorbed that.

"I especially don't want Ben to screw up the best thing that ever happened to him."

"I was that best thing?"

"Always. Well, Ben is now, but yeah, you were. You were the only woman I ever loved. Too bad there's no way to go back in time."

"No, but if there were, you wouldn't have Ben. Or your own business."

His shrug was bittersweet. "And you wouldn't be a doctor. Funny how things turn out."

"We play the cards we are dealt, even when the hand sucks," Chandy said, using one of Chase's lines. "Hopefully we win a few now and then."

"I wish I would have known you were pregnant."

"I wish you would have called me before I knew."

In the distance they could hear the sounds of birds and of children laughing.

"I guess we're at an impasse," Justin said.

"We can wonder 'what if' the rest of our days..." Chandy began.

"Or take things from here," he finished.

Her mood was sad and quiet, and they sat in silence, again registering the distant joyous cries of children. She realized she hadn't asked him where Ben was. Probably home with his grandmother, like Chris's kids. They were much more interested in playing video games than gathering Easter eggs.

"So where do we go from here?" Justin prompted.

She watched a few egg hunters who had already filled their baskets walk toward their cars. "I don't know. My grandfather thinks you're bad for me."

"He never did like me much," Justin mused.

"Don't take it personally. He never liked anyone after you, either. I'm his little princess."

"And because he loved you he put up with me."

She nodded. "Yes."

"Do you believe in second chances?"

"I don't know."

He reached for her hands. "Let's find out. Let's start over. I'd very much like to see you again, and not just because I have your car held hostage."

A light breeze wafted under the overhang and into the gazebo. The air was ripe with spring. But it was Justin's words that had caused the catch in her breath. "You mean that? You really want to try again?"

"Yes. You're a beautiful and successful woman. I'm even more intrigued by you now than I was fifteen years ago. I would so much like another chance to get to know you."

"Oh." Her heart fluttered. He was like her grandfather in his directness. Justin moved closer, but retained a respectable distance, one that wouldn't have the Chenille matrons' tongues wagging about inappropriateness.

"We're adults now, Chandy. We have a past, and a sad one at that. But our past doesn't mean we can't have a shot at the present. Abby and Richard? They didn't reconnect until five years ago, and they rediscovered their love. There's hope for us, too. We can rekindle what we once had, or even find something better. We won't know until we try. Let's get to know each other. Hang out over pizza, go see a movie."

She thought about that. The idea of dating Justin was startling yet oddly welcome. She was attracted to the man next to her. He was handsome, kind and loving, and a good father.

But how did she open her heart to the one who'd hurt her? Did it start with forgiveness? She couldn't have kids because of him. But somehow her earlier rage had faded. "So how do you know that about Richard and Abby?"

"I'm actually a client of Richard's."

"You seem to know everyone."

"He's in sales. Tools. I buy them for my shop."

"Amazing."

After missing Justin for fifteen years, she realized that they'd been connected in a way, through the people they knew. It was all a bit overwhelming.

Chandy shifted and put her chin in her hands. "What

if things don't work out? I don't think I could handle you breaking my heart again."

"Let me assure you that's the last thing I want. I wouldn't be able to live with myself if I hurt you again. So how about we take things slow? It's not like when we were in high school and we couldn't see past tomorrow. We don't have to go steady after two weeks."

She laughed at that. "Yeah. Life was much more intense then. Now we have the perspective of age and experience."

"Exactly. So how about we start with one date? If it doesn't go well, we'll agree to be good friends. I'd like to be your friend, Chandy, even if the romance doesn't work."

His proposition sounded so reasonable. After all, what could one date hurt? She bit her lower lip, needing a few more safety nets.

"Will you let me pick the date? What we do? Where we go?"

His blue eyes twinkled "Sure. Didn't you always, with a few exceptions?"

"I believe I did." Her earlier sour mood vanished. The world seemed full of promise and a rare, giddy feeling took over. A date with Justin. Somewhere deep inside, a part of her whispered *dumb idea* but Chandy ignored that inner voice and trusted the instincts that said *go for it.*

After all, she'd lost all she could lose. There was nothing else he could take from her.

"Then, Justin McCall, yes. You've got yourself one date."

Chapter Six

The weekend after Easter, Chandy still hadn't decided what to do about her date with Justin. When she'd said she'd pick the spot, she hadn't realized how difficult organizing a date would be.

Because the more she thought about their date, the more she wanted something perfect. Something special. For whatever reason, going on this date was suddenly very important. She'd tried to analyze why, and simply given up. She'd thought about calling a therapist, but decided that she was ready to handle things on her own. It just was important to her, and that was a good enough reason.

Although that attitude had created her current dilemma. Every idea she'd come up with for the date, and every idea Paige had suggested, Chandy had tossed out as unworthy.

One date. That was all she and Justin were giving themselves. If it went wrong, well, that was it. And even though they hadn't had their date yet, it wasn't as if she and Justin weren't talking.

Once back from Iowa, their reconnection had started

with one phone call from Justin. Then two. Then three. They'd gabbed over three hours until late at night, stopping only when the batteries on their phones were exhausted. During the day they sent each other texts.

They talked and texted about things like old friends. He told her how Ben's ball season was going. They discussed television shows. Movies. She loved the phone calls best because she liked to listen to his deep, sexy voice. His laugh could give her happy goose bumps. He'd told her he couldn't wait to kiss her.

She wanted the same thing, and wondered how the touch of his lips would make her feel. Craig's brief kisses had done nothing. No zip. No zing. Chandy suspected that wasn't going to be a problem with Justin.

Her phone beeped, indicating she had a text. Only the baby she rocked kept her from grabbing for her cell and reading it.

"I have to get my head on straight," she told the eight-month-old she held in her lap. As he was sleeping, he didn't reply. Chandy sighed, thinking she had to be the silliest person on the planet.

She was long over the days when she'd run home to see if the answering machine light blinked. But this new friendship with Justin made her feel special, and it had been a long time since she'd felt that way. He hadn't pressed for details of the date, either, which surprised her.

He was respecting her space, giving her time. While in high school he'd done that in regards to sex, with most other things he'd liked an immediate answer. But this older, more mature Justin had learned patience in all things. She liked him even more for that.

She passed the sleeping baby to the nurse. Chandy had a rare Saturday off, and she'd spent the morning at the crisis nursery. Now she was off to lunch with Paige.

She met Paige in Old Webster, an area of Webster Groves around Elm and Lockwood. Since the weather was warm and sunny, they sat at the bistro tables located along the sidewalk.

"So what did you have to tell me?" Chandy asked after their salads arrived. They'd been chatting about all sorts of things lately, but Paige had mentioned a small problem when she'd called to suggest lunch. "Are Ahmed's parents fighting again?" Chandy asked.

Paige shook her head. "No, thank goodness. That marriage counseling they've been doing has really helped. It's been a year since they almost divorced. So far so good."

Paige toyed with her glass of iced tea. "I'm just worried about my own marriage."

Chandy instantly put down her fork so she could give Paige her full attention. "What's going on? What happened?"

Paige drummed her fingers on the table, a clear sign she was upset. "The problem's me. Remember how I told you Ahmed and I had agreed that we didn't want kids?"

"Yeah." Chandy had a feeling she already knew what Paige was going to say.

"Well, I'm pregnant. I saw the doctor Friday and

he confirmed everything. Now I just have to tell my husband. He's going to freak out. I'm forty. Ahmed's forty-five. We weren't planning this, obviously. He's going to flip. He's always been so adamant that no kids was the way to go."

Chandy gave Paige's hand a sympathetic squeeze. "Think positive. He might respond better than you think. Anyway, the important thing is, how do you feel about this baby?"

Paige gave a wry smile. "Nervous. I don't know anything about being a mother. I was an only child, my cousins lived two states away and I never even babysat. What if I can't do this?"

Chandy worked to reassure her friend. "Well, let's see. Unlike all those people who probably shouldn't have children for one reason or another, you have a good job and a great husband. You're smart and kind and loving. I think you're going to be a great mother."

"Really?" Paige's eyes widened hopefully.

"Yes, and I think Ahmed's going to be thrilled. It'll be a change and an adjustment. But you have the room in your house. Just make sure he doesn't have to give up his cars."

"Ahmed loves his cars."

"Exactly. If he gives even a tenth of that love to a child, and you know he's going to give much more, you're in great shape. Besides, remember your cancer? Your fears were unjustified then."

Paige laughed. "True. I really get myself down by stressing. I probably have nothing to worry about."

"Exactly. So how are you going to tell him?"

"I thought I'd take him out of town. You know, one of those spur-of-the-moment romantic weekends. We have those Cardinals tickets next Saturday night, but we see enough games that we can miss one. Hey, do you want them?"

"What? The tickets?"

"Yes. Your seats aren't up for a while and Ahmed and I have four we won't be using that night. Why don't you take Justin and Ben? Go on that date you've been putting off."

Chandy thought about that for a moment. She and Justin both loved baseball. And as she'd bought into season tickets with others, Paige was right—she wouldn't be seeing a game in her own seats for a while. "Is it really a date if we take Ben along? We only are giving ourselves one."

"So change the rules and make it two. And why not take Ben? He and his dad are sort of a package deal. And there are four seats, so Ben could bring a friend. It's the perfect setup."

"Maybe. I was envisioning something more romantic."

Paige's brow creased and her lips puckered. "Oh, please. You haven't thought of anything yet, and these are the green seats behind home plate. That means dinner in the club beforehand."

"That is pretty special. Okay. You know how much I love baseball and I can't pass up those seats. So what do I owe you?"

"Not a thing. Don't even try to protest."

"Thank you. That's generous."

"It's what friends do. Besides, I appreciate you listening to me."

"Which is also what friends do. You know I'm thrilled for you. I'll have to throw you a baby shower."

Paige patted her stomach. "I'm not sure about all this, but life is about change, you know?"

Chandy nodded. "Yeah," she agreed, thinking of her upcoming date. "It is."

CHANDY PICKED UP HER CELL phone to call Justin. She was back at her condo, extremely full because both women had decided to indulge in dessert. They'd split a piece of chocolate cake, which really had been too large for one person anyway.

Justin picked up on the first ring. "Hey, how are you?" he asked, his baritone sending little shivers along her skin.

"Good. I just had lunch with Paige."

"And how is she?"

"Fine. In fact, that's why I'm calling. Paige offered me her Cardinals tickets for next Saturday. She and Ahmed have four. They were thinking of inviting friends, but now she's taking him out of town instead. She's telling him some important news over a romantic getaway in Chicago."

"Wow." The phone grew silent as Justin absorbed everything. "She's pregnant?"

"Yes. You won't tell Ahmed, will you?"

"Of course not! The secret's safe with me."

"Good. I'm so thrilled for her. Anyway, I'd like to

take you and Ben, and one of Ben's friends, to the ball game."

"We'd love to go."

"You would?" she asked.

"Yeah. We're free. Ben doesn't have a game that day, and it's been too long. I'd like to see you."

"Me, too." A weight lifted off Chandy's shoulders and her fingers relaxed. "This isn't what I'd planned but we all love baseball and…"

"It'll be a good date. Tell Paige I'm happy to pay for the tickets."

"Oh, no. I already offered and Paige refuses to take anything for them. They're actually Ahmed's parents' seats, but they split them. Dinner's included."

"Where are these seats?"

"They're the green ones behind home plate. I sat there once and it was amazing. I'd love to share that experience with you and Ben."

"Well, then how can we pass it up?"

"You can't." Chandy laughed.

THE WEEK FLEW BY QUICKLY. Justin had insisted he drive to Busch Stadium, and he picked her up at 4:00 p.m.

"I can't believe Paige and Ahmed have these seats," Ben said. They'd arrived in time to see player warm-ups and to have dinner.

"Well, they are the last row in the section," Chandy said.

Ben shot her a look that said he thought she might be crazy, and Chandy laughed. Ben had brought his best friend, Andy, and both guys were in awe of sitting in the stadium's high-rent district. During practice, fans often moved closer to the wall by the Cardinals dugout. Ben and Andy had joined the small crowd and were each able to get several autographs.

At dinner, they enjoyed steak and lobster. Ben and Andy recognized several local business leaders at nearby tables from a television news project they'd had to do for social studies class.

"I could get used to this," Justin said in the top of the fifth inning when the waitstaff brought him his second and last beer of the night, also included in the ticket price. He glanced around. "So where are your seats?"

"Up there," Chandy said. "I'm in the Red Bird club. Not as fancy, and pay-as-you-go."

"Still, better than what I have, which is no season tickets at all." Justin squeezed her hand. "Thank you for thinking of me and Ben when Paige offered. This is a rare treat for us."

"Hang with me and maybe you can come again," she teased.

His forehead creased and his mood darkened. "I'm not here with you for that," Justin said, his voice quiet and serious.

"Huh?" Chandy replied. She'd been joking. She turned toward him. The Cardinals were already up by four, and the opposing team was changing pitchers. Ben and Andy had taken the opportunity to find the men's room.

Justin took another sip of beer. Then he exhaled and spoke slowly, as if carefully choosing his words. "I don't want you to think we only came tonight because you had great seats. I'm not with you because you have money and connections."

"I never thought that." Her words came out clipped.

He clenched his hands together. "I'm screwing this up again, like I seem to do every time I talk to you about something important. I just want you to know that I'm very aware of our financial differences, and I'm not a gold digger."

She placed her hand on his, her touch reassuring. "I never thought you were."

"Good. As long as that's clear."

Ben and Andy returned, interrupting the conversation. The first Cardinals batter came up to the plate, leaving Chandy to her thoughts. She hadn't expected this, hadn't really considered the disparity in their financial situations at all.

She could understand Justin's position; after all, she'd seen the price on the tickets, too. Paige had been quite generous. The evening had been perfect, so far. The Arch twinkled in the distance, and her favorite team was winning. Nothing, she determined, was going to ruin this night.

But the dynamic had changed. And although the shift in Justin's attitude was so slight that Ben and Andy didn't notice anything, Chandy did. Even after so many years apart, she recognized the tightness of his jaw that told her something was wrong, besides the fact that the New York Mets had eaten the Cardinals' lead, and the game was tied at 7–7.

He was used to being a provider, and he had always

insisted on paying for their dates no matter how many times she'd offered during their relationship. He was old-fashioned that way. She sighed, realizing this was another conversation they would have to have.

The ninth inning arrived, and the Cardinals kept the Mets from scoring. But as the Cardinals also failed to get any runs, it took two extra innings before a home run gave the Redbirds the victory they needed.

"That was such a great game! Thanks again for taking me," Andy said as they stood to go.

"Me, too," Ben added, remembering his manners, as they began to make their way out of the stadium.

Chandy paused when she saw a souvenir stand. "Oh, wait. I told Chris I'd get something for my nephews the next time I was here. Hold on."

Everyone followed her to the rolling kiosks. "Sorry, I should have done this earlier."

"It's fine," Justin said. "Traffic's going to be a nightmare no matter when we leave."

"Traffic is always bad," Chandy agreed. "Waiting won't hurt."

She perused the items, selecting two ball caps and several commemorative pins. She heard Andy and Ben discussing some items over on the next cart, and glanced over to see Cardinals baseball jackets similar to those the players wore when it was chilly. "Those are nice. Do you think my nephews would like them instead?"

"I would. I've been trying to get my dad to buy me one. He said maybe for my next birthday," Ben replied, tugging on his Cardinals ball cap.

"What about the pennants?" Chandy asked, pointing at some.

"Yeah, those are cool, too," Ben replied.

The pennants didn't cost much, so Chandy bought four. She also purchased two coats in addition to the hats and pins. As the vendor swiped her credit card, she handed a pennant to Ben and one to Andy. "A souvenir so you can remember tonight."

"Thanks," Ben said. She overheard him telling Andy a few minutes later how awesome he thought she was.

Justin took her bags as they made their way to the reserved parking lot. Ben and Andy climbed into the back of the SUV as he opened the tailgate and put her stuff inside. She waited as Justin closed the tailgate and then handed him a small brown paper bag.

"What's this?"

"Just a little something. I saw it and thought of you."

Justin peered into the bag. Inside was one of the Cardinals collector pins. He took it out.

"I remember how you used to collect these. You had a few from that trip to Disneyland. And one from the Twins game, remember?"

He stared at the pin, and then his hand closed around it. "Thanks."

She frowned. "What's wrong?"

He shook his head. "Nothing. Let's get going."

He followed her around to the passenger side and opened her door. She strapped in and turned to the guys, who had pulled their iPods and their phones out, their thumbs already texting and music playing in their ears. Justin climbed in and started the car.

"They're already zoned out," Chandy remarked.

He nodded and began to back out of the parking space. "Yep. That's typical. Earbuds in, music on. You'd think they'd have a conversation, but they probably missed a bunch of texts during the ball game. They can't resist the urge any longer."

Justin had insisted the boys actually turn off their phones during the game, not just put them on silent. They'd been so into the game they hadn't cared.

"It's such a different world from when we were kids," Chandy said. "Imagine what would have happened if you and I could have texted. Or e-mailed. Or sent messages on Facebook."

"Yeah, maybe things would have worked out differently for us."

They were still sitting in traffic, having gotten out of the parking lot and onto the street. "So tell me what's bothering you," she pressed.

He kept his eyes on the road. "Nothing. Let's not ruin tonight." He gave her a smile. "It's all past and we said we weren't going back there."

She studied his profile. "Maybe we were wrong about that. Maybe we have to deal with some of it in order to move on."

His fingers flexed on the steering wheel. "You didn't need to buy me anything."

"It was nothing." She glanced over her shoulder, but no one in the backseat was paying any attention to what was going on in the front.

"Chandy, all those pins I used to collect are gone. My uncle threw them away one day when he was drunk."

She reached over and put a hand on his thigh. "Hey, it's okay. Pin one. Starting over."

"Yeah." The traffic began moving as the light changed and he focused on driving. After he made a right turn and the highway entrance ramp became visible, he took a deep breath and finally spoke.

"Look, I'm sorry. I don't mean to be a downer. Tonight has been special, but it's also proven that we're very different. All my spare change goes to Ben's college fund and the price of your car could cover four years of state school tuition. Chandy, I like you, but at the same time, what can I give you?"

"Yourself?"

"Is that going to be enough? You run in a different crowd, live in a different world."

"Not all doctors are rich. You'd be amazed at how much money it costs to run an office. That's why so many doctors form groups. The malpractice insurance costs alone are through the roof."

Justin tried to make her understand. "I'm not saying it's not a struggle or that there aren't bills to pay. What I'm saying is that people like me can't afford to buy and customize new Porsches or spring for season tickets. Already Ben wants his own car when he turns sixteen, but that's not happening. If there's a time when we need two cars, he can use the shop's loaner."

"So can we get past this?" she asked.

"I want to."

They'd hit the interstate, but traffic was still heavy

FREE Merchandise is 'in the Cards' for you!

Dear Reader,

We're giving away FREE MERCHANDISE!

Seriously, we'd like to reward you for reading this novel by giving you **FREE MERCHANDISE** worth over **$20**. And no purchase is necessary!

You see the Jack of Hearts sticker above? Paste that sticker in the box on the Free Merchandise Voucher inside. Return the Voucher promptly...and we'll send you valuable Free Merchandise!

Thanks again for reading one of our novels—and enjoy your Free Merchandise with our compliments!

Pam Powers

Pam Powers

P.S. Look inside to see what Free Merchandise is **"in the cards"** for you!

(H-AR-09/10)

YOUR FREE MERCHANDISE INCLUDES...

2 FREE Harlequin® American Romance Books

AND 2 FREE Mystery Gifts

FREE MERCHANDISE VOUCHER

2 FREE BOOKS and **2 FREE GIFTS**

Please send my Free Merchandise, consisting of
2 Free Books and **2 Free Mystery Gifts**.
I understand that I am under no obligation to buy
anything, as explained on the back of this card.

*About how many NEW paperback fiction books
have you purchased in the past 3 months?*

☐ 0-2   ☐ 3-6   ☐ 7 or more
E7L6   E7MJ   E7MU

154/354 HDL

Please Print

FIRST NAME

LAST NAME

ADDRESS

APT.#   CITY

STATE/PROV.   ZIP/POSTAL CODE

Offer limited to one per household and not valid to current subscribers of Harlequin® American Romance books.
Your Privacy—Harlequin Books is committed to protecting your privacy. Our Privacy Policy is available online at
www.ReaderService.com or upon request from the Reader Service. From time to time we make our lists of
customers available to reputable third parties who may have a product or service of interest to you. If you would
prefer for us not to share your name and address, please check here ☐. **Help us get it right**—We strive for
accurate, respectful and relevant communications. To clarify or modify your communication preferences, visit us at
www.ReaderService.com/consumerchoice.

NO PURCHASE NECESSARY!

▼ Detach card and mail today. No stamp needed. ▼

© 2010 HARLEQUIN ENTERPRISES LIMITED • and ™ are trademarks owned and used by the trademark owner and/or its licensee. Printed in the U.S.A.

(H-AR-09/10)

The Reader Service - Here's how it works:

Accepting your 2 free books and 2 free mystery gifts (gifts valued at approximately $10.00) places you under no obligation to buy anything. You may keep the books and gifts and return the shipping statement marked "cancel." If you do not cancel, about a month later we'll send you 4 additional books and bill you just $4.24 each in the U.S. or $4.99 each in Canada. That's a savings of 15% off the cover price. It's quite a bargain! Shipping and handling is just 50¢ per book. * You may cancel at any time, but if you choose to continue, every month we'll send you 4 more books, which you may either purchase at the discount price or return to us and cancel your subscription.

* Terms and prices subject to change without notice. Prices do not include applicable taxes. Sales tax applicable in N.Y. Canadian residents will be charged applicable provincial taxes and GST. Offer not valid in Quebec. All orders subject to approval. Books received may not be as shown. Credit or debit balances in a customer's account(s) may be offset by any other outstanding balance owed by or to the customer. Please allow 4 to 6 weeks for delivery. Offer available while quantities last.

▲ If offer card is missing write to: The Reader Service, P.O. Box 1867, Buffalo, NY 14240-1867 or visit www.ReaderService.com ▲

BUSINESS REPLY MAIL
FIRST-CLASS MAIL   PERMIT NO. 717   BUFFALO, NY

POSTAGE WILL BE PAID BY ADDRESSEE

THE READER SERVICE
PO BOX 1867
BUFFALO NY 14240-9952

NO POSTAGE
NECESSARY
IF MAILED
IN THE
UNITED STATES

as cars divided, some to Highway 55 southbound, or others, like Justin, onto Highway 44 westbound. She patted his leg. "I'm here because I want to be."

"Okay." He covered her hand with his own.

She suddenly understood that if she wanted this relationship, she needed to try to understand where Justin was coming from. He was the type who was too proud to take anything from anyone. Sure, he had a few business loans, but he didn't sponge or accept charity.

Chandy's grandparents always made sure she had everything she wanted or needed. She knew she'd been spoiled.

As they passed the Kingshighway exit, a voice called out from the backseat, interrupting the silence. "Hey, Dad, can we stop at Ted Drewes?"

Ted Drewes was an ice cream shop on the old historic Route 66. A permanent fixture in St. Louis, the store sold what locals called frozen custard or, in slang terms, concrete. Basically, the ice cream was so thick you could turn over the cup with the contents inside and the spoon wouldn't fall out.

"Is that okay with you?" Justin asked.

"I'd love some," Chandy said.

"We'll stop then. Since Andy's spending the night at our house, we've got time."

"Cool." Ben put his earbuds back in.

Justin exited at Hampton, made a right onto Watson and another right onto Chippewa. They found a parking spot and joined the queue at Ted Drewes. Once they'd gotten their ice cream, Justin popped open the tailgate and he and Chandy sat on the back. Ben and Andy lingered nearby, people watching and commenting on girls. Many St. Louis natives even had the lawn chairs out, while others sat on the curb. Ted Drewes was an institution.

"Mmm. I don't get down here much anymore," Justin admitted. "When I first moved to St. Louis I came here all the time. I lived just a few streets over on Loughborough."

"Since St. Louis University's not too far away, we used to come here all the time."

She'd only ordered a mini concrete, but the guys had gotten larges, so they took longer to eat their ice cream. She glanced around, seeing bugs already swarming the light poles—a sure sign that although it was May, summer was on its way. Chandy grinned. That was another thing St. Louis was known for—bugs and skipping spring.

But summer hadn't arrived yet, and she shivered slightly as the cool breeze picked up. She'd forgotten to bring a jacket. "Hey, are you cold?" Justin asked.

"A little. Probably also the ice cream effect. You know, whenever you eat ice cream you get a little chill?"

He shrugged out of his denim jacket and placed it over her shoulders like he'd done in high school. Chandy had worn his letterman jacket more than he had. She sniffed—the jacket smelled of Justin, and the scent was familiar but different. She immediately felt warmer and safer and he tugged the sides around her, wrapping the jacket tighter.

"Better?" he asked. He'd moved closer when he'd

given her the jacket, and she looked up into his face. His lips tempted her.

"Yes," she breathed. "But we have a bit of an audience." Ben and Andy had gone up to the side of the building where Ted Drewes had cups and water. They were lingering, trying to give the adults space.

"Ben's probably surprised. As I said, I don't date much, and there have only been a few rare times that I've ever brought anyone around."

"How rare?"

"I can count them on one hand. If the relationship wasn't serious, I kept the woman away from Ben. I didn't want him getting too attached to anyone."

"Aren't you afraid he'll get attached to me?"

Justin sighed. "Very, but you're different. I figure I'll just have to deal with consequences. Despite our incomes and everything, I don't want just one date."

Her gaze held his. She had no idea whether they could make things work, but she wanted to try. "Me neither."

The boys began to walk back over, ready to go home to video games and more texting. Once they were in the car, they put their headphones in again and ignored the adults.

It took about twenty minutes to reach Chandy's condo. Justin walked her to her door and waited while she removed her house key. The boys were out of view.

"I had a nice time tonight," he said.

"Isn't that supposed to be my line?"

He grinned. "Maybe, but I wanted you to know."

"Let's see where things lead," Chandy replied.

"So a second date?"

"Agreed."

He rubbed the pad of his forefinger on her bottom lip, making it tingle. "May I say good-night with a kiss?"

She was moved that he'd asked. Craig had simply assumed she'd let him kiss her, which had made for a very awkward moment the first time he'd leaned in and she'd backed up.

But this was Justin, the guy who'd given her her very first kiss, if you didn't count that two-second lip-lock in kindergarten with Billy Kneese out on the playground after someone had dared them.

"Please," she said simply, and Justin edged forward, a piece of his light brown hair falling toward his eye as his mouth descended. His lips touched hers, the pressure light and tentative. Then suddenly the kiss was like coming home. As if her body recognized the only man she had ever truly cared about.

Chandy's eyes closed as Justin deepened the kiss. There were no words to describe the sheer joy of such a simple kiss that conveyed everything.

Her arms went around his neck. His hands encircled her waist. A current passed between them, but unlike fifteen years ago, this sensation wasn't teen hormones. The desire had matured like a fine wine. She could taste the difference, and it was decadent. Sweet. Intoxicating.

If Ben hadn't honked the horn, the sound echoing down the street, she could have stood on her front porch step and kissed Justin forever. Instead he drew away. "I'm going to kill that kid," he mumbled.

"Not on my account," Chandy said, missing his lips already.

"No, on mine. He'll be lucky to live past the next five minutes."

Justin raked a hand through his hair, and then he leaned down to give her a quick peck on the cheek. "Okay, I guess I'd better take the boys home. I'll call you tomorrow."

"I'll look forward to it." She stood there, waiting.

He shifted and put his hands in his pockets. "Go inside so I know you're safe."

He'd been like that years ago, never leaving until she was behind the closed door. She resisted the urge to claim another quick kiss and put her key in the lock. She went inside and immediately peered out the front windows, where she had a brief view of Justin driving away.

He'd kissed her. Her knees gave out with the enormity of what had occurred and she sat on the couch. She pressed her lips, feeling their slight puffiness. *Magical* didn't even come close to describing the kiss.

Ten minutes later, her phone rang and she answered. "I couldn't wait until tomorrow to call," Justin said. "I had fun. Good night and sleep tight."

"I will." She hung up then, and held the phone to her chest. For the first time in years she felt a sense of promise. That somehow everything would turn out well.

She moved her legs, tapping her feet on the floor as

a giddiness overtook her. She smiled at Mr. Wu, who came over for a head scratch. She couldn't have kids, and had long ago learned adoption wasn't viable. Still, maybe she could have the rest.

Chapter Seven

The next day dawned clear and bright. A sunbeam cut across Chandy's bed, but it wasn't the light waking her this Sunday morning.

Her hand smacked the bedside table several times as she groped for her cell phone. Today was her day off, but that didn't mean anything. Eyes still trying to focus, she pressed a button and put the phone to her ear. "Hello?"

"Good morning. Don't you sound all wide-awake and chipper?" Justin's warm voice resonated in her ear.

"Still asleep," she mumbled.

"It's after ten."

That made her sit. The bedside clock confirmed it. Ten-fifteen. "I never sleep this late!"

"Then you must have needed the shut-eye. I'm in the neighborhood. Thought I'd drop by if that's okay. I'll bring you breakfast and pick up my jacket."

"Now?" Chandy squeaked. The mirror over her dresser told her what a bad idea that was. Her hair stood straight up. She needed a shower. She put a hand over her mouth and grimaced. Bad morning breath. She was far from presentable.

"Well, since you aren't up, how about an hour from now? Instead of breakfast, I'll take you to lunch."

An hour was much more reasonable. Her stomach growled its acceptance. "Is Ben with you?"

"Nope. Andy went home and Ben went to Six Flags with his friend Jake. The park won't close until six. Since I've got the day free, I risked it and called. I will understand if you can't see me."

"No, an hour's great."

"Sure that's enough time?"

"Yes." Unlike a roommate she'd had in college who'd needed at least a full hour before she could go anywhere, Chandy could be showered and ready to leave in under twenty minutes. An hour would give her time to spare.

"I'll see you soon then," Justin said.

"Sounds good." Chandy disconnected and, twenty-five minutes later, walked into her kitchen. She'd showered and dressed, choosing a lightweight red sweater and a pair of chino walking shorts. She fed the cat, poured herself a glass of orange juice and checked her e-mail. Her phone rang as she was reading one of those "Twenty things you didn't know about me" notes on Facebook. "Hey, are you running late?" she asked, not checking the number.

"Not that I know of," her brother Chase said.

"Oh. Hey." *Oops.*

"Expecting someone else I take it," Chase said. "Is it a guy?"

"Yeah. We're going to lunch."

"And since you're not telling me his name, let me guess. Justin."

"So what if it is? It's just lunch. Anyway, what's going on?"

"I need to know if you're planning on coming up to the lake for Leroy's birthday party. Miranda and I want to do something special since he's turning eighty-five. But we aren't planning anything as elaborate as his eightieth birthday party."

"Hard to believe you two met five years ago and first got to know each other at that party," Chandy mused.

"Yep. It's an anniversary of sorts for us, too." Chase was reflective for a moment and then got back to business. "So we can count on you to be there?"

"Of course. I've only missed two of his birthdays and that was when I was doing my residency," she replied, irritated that Chase would even ask.

"Will Justin be coming?"

"I don't know. Isn't that rather soon?"

"Maybe, but then again my wife says I have no clue about these things and that I'm lucky to have her."

"She's right."

"She's the one who told me to ask you. So is it serious?"

"We've had one date. We went to a ball game last night. He's sweet and kind and he really regrets his behavior as a teenager. People change, Chase. You certainly have."

She'd gotten him with that, and he groaned again. "True."

Chandy's front doorbell rang. "Gotta go." She hung up and closed her laptop. She met Justin at the front door, her purse in one hand and his denim jacket in the other. She'd been so cozy, she'd forgotten to give it back to him last night. He'd dressed in jeans and a polo shirt and he held out a cup of coffee. "Thanks," she said, swapping the coat for the java.

"You're welcome."

Chandy followed him down the front walk. She glanced around for the car she'd been in last night, but didn't see it. "Where's your car?"

He pointed down the block a bit, to a vintage Corvette. "Right over there."

She whistled. "Nice. That's yours?"

He beamed, pride evident. "Yep. A 1969. I found her in a junkyard. You should have seen the shape she was in. Took me five years to finish her and get her running." He opened the passenger door. "Your chariot awaits."

Chandy balanced her purse and the coffee Justin had given her as she climbed in. Everything was meticulously done. He slid into the driver's seat and turned the key.

"Did you do all the work yourself?"

"Most of it. I'm not that good at the mechanical things so one of the guys in the shop did that work. But I did all the body work and paint myself."

"I like it," Chandy said as the engine began to purr. "A Corvette always was one of your dream cars."

"I know I always said I wanted a big muscle car, but when I saw this I couldn't believe my eyes. It was like a needle in a haystack or a diamond in the rough. Cost me five hundred since she was junked. The rest I did as I could, figuring she'd be proof of the work my shop could do once I'd finished her. Technically she belongs to the business."

He patted the black dashboard. "She's proof you can restore anything."

Chandy took his words as a good omen. Maybe they could restore their relationship, recapture the magic they'd had, only in a different and even better way. The day was warm, so Justin had removed the T-tops. A light breeze blew Chandy's hair as they drove down the street. She loved it.

They headed west on Highway 64 toward Chesterfield, crossed the Daniel Boone Bridge over the Missouri River and then decided to take Highway 94 south. The road played host to several wineries, and they chose one overlooking a scenic hillside.

They sat at a table out in the sun, but far enough away from the stage so that the band playing classic rock music didn't drown out their conversation.

Justin held out his wineglass. "Cheers."

"Cheers," Chandy replied, clinking her glass against his. They'd ordered a bottle of Seyval, a semisweet vintage, and they had one of the winery's signature pizzas on the way. She sipped the wine. Delicious. "Good idea for lunch."

"Thanks for joining me. Today seemed like a good day for a road trip. I've been here once before. Some friends had their wedding reception in that barn over there. It was pretty cool."

"What was your wedding like?"

Justin's face clouded. "Nothing like that. We went to the courthouse and signed on the dotted line. The marriage was over about a week later, but we didn't officially divorce until after Ben was born. Really, it was a mistake from the get-go."

"You only married her because she was pregnant."

"Yeah. I wanted to do the right thing." He reached for her hand. "Let's dance."

"But our pizza…"

"We'll see the waitress when she brings it out." He was already on his feet, guiding her upward. He led her over to the wooden, ground level deck that served as a dance floor. The beautiful May weather had everyone outside, and as most wineries in the area celebrated Maifest every weekend in May, the dance floor was full of revelers. He drew her close and twirled her once when they had room.

She laughed as she caught his foot. "We never were good at this."

"Then we need to practice." He spun her again, this time pulling her to his chest as he brought her around. The world faded away as his lips descended on hers.

Like their kiss the previous night, this one was sweet and gentle. Yet fueled by desire the kiss became something more—the promise of a fresh start.

The band changed tempos, speeding up to play "Shout" and as the dance floor became crowded again, Justin ended the kiss and led Chandy toward the table. "Our pizza's coming," he told her.

The waitress reached the table the same time they did, and set down a large thin-crust hamburger, onions and pepperoni pizza. Chandy reached for an edge piece, while Justin took one from the middle.

"You still favor the outside and I want the inside," he said, dumping Parmesan cheese on his piece before folding it in half. "That's why we're so compatible."

He tilted his head, studied her for a minute. "One question. Do you hog the remote?"

She used a knife and fork, and lifted the morsel she'd cut to her mouth. "It's my house. Of course I do."

He laughed at that, and she finished her slice, amazed at the ease at which they were falling back into sync. Long ago she and Justin had even finished each other's sentences. They had communicated on a level intrinsic to only them. The more time they spent together, the more they fell into their former rhythm.

"Is everything okay here?" The waitress was back.

"It's great," Chandy replied. They'd eaten most of the pizza and polished off half a bottle of wine. They'd each had about two glasses since their arrival at the winery, so they capped the bottle and rejoined the crowd on the dance floor.

Justin kept one hand on her at all times, and during slow numbers he'd put his arms around her waist and hold her tight.

The band finished its final set, and Chandy and Justin were surprised the afternoon had slipped away. They returned to their table where they had a pitcher of water and some of the winery's famous sugar cookies waiting.

"So back to work tomorrow," Justin said.

"Yes," Chandy replied. "But it'll go quickly. It's

almost Memorial Day weekend. I'm taking a few days off and heading to Minnesota for my grandfather's birthday."

"Ah, the infamous lake house that you always disappeared to each summer."

"That's the one." She fingered the edge of a paper napkin before looking him in the eye. She loved the lake, but once she'd started dating, going to the lake had meant being apart from Justin. "You and Ben should come with me, see what the fuss is all about."

Justin shook his head. "Your grandfather wouldn't like that. Besides, I'm not sure I'm comfortable with the idea."

"Justin, if we want to make this work, you need to accept that some things are simply a part of me. I can't help that I'm a McDaniel."

"True."

"Dating me again means you're going to have to leave your comfort zone. My family has money, yes. I can afford to buy myself a fancy car. But I'm me. I'm a package. Just like you and Ben are a package."

"I know. I'm intimidated, that's all. Your grandfather's pretty scary."

"He can be daunting, but this isn't about him. It's all about what you and I want. The external stuff doesn't matter. It's who you are inside that makes you special. So let's not worry about my grandfather, or my family, or my money. Let's just be us."

"I do want this."

"And I want you," Chandy said. She knew she'd have

some groundwork to lay first, but figured she could do that in a phone call to her grandfather.

"So shall we do date number three?" Justin asked.

"Definitely. But don't be dating anyone else on the side. I'm not like that."

She was teasing, but he grabbed her hand and held it tight. "There's no one else. Besides, I never could look at another girl when I was with you."

A shiver of delight raced up her back. "Really?"

"Yep. I'll repeat it again. You've always been the only woman for me. There's never been anyone else who captured had my heart like you did."

"Ditto." The word slipped out so easily, and even more amazing was how fast Justin moved. His lips were on hers in a heartbeat. She reveled in the moment, the world again fading into the background as if she and Justin were the only two people who mattered.

They stood there, oblivious, until the sound of clinking glasses, chairs shuffling and gravel crunching began to intrude. Most wineries in the area closed at five, which was in ten minutes. "Time to go," Justin said.

They held hands all the way to the car, and soon were winding their way farther south on Highway 94, taking the long way home. They crossed the Missouri River again, this time into historic Washington. They cruised the riverfront and drove by the city fairgrounds.

"Maybe we should go out to Hermann sometime."

Hermann was a small river-town west of Washington, known for its wineries and bed-and-breakfasts. "I'd like that," Chandy replied. But for today they headed east, toward home.

The drive back seemed faster, and it was just after six when they arrived at Chandy's doorstep.

"Thanks for joining me," Justin said.

"Are you coming in?" She couldn't believe how much she wanted him to. She didn't want the night to end.

"No." He leaned in to kiss her forehead. "I have to get Ben from his friend's and make sure he studies for his finals, which start Tuesday. He's finished with school this week."

A lump lodged in her throat. She was disappointed, but she understood. "I hated finals."

"Me, too."

"You'll think about Minnesota?"

"I'll think about it, but let's see each other this week. I'm playing Ahmed's team in softball on Tuesday night. It's a six-o'clock game. Maybe you could come and hang out with Paige but cheer for me."

"I could probably do that. I should be done at work by five."

"Then let's make it a plan," he said, and then he gave her another long kiss that sent her spiraling. She wrapped her arms around his neck, wanting never to let go. But soon he was stepping away, and she was in her house alone, as if the magic had never happened.

Mr. Wu started meowing once she got inside, craving food and attention. Chandy gave him both and settled down to watch a show she'd recorded. Whenever she traveled, the girl a few doors down would pet-sit. She made a mental note to call her. At that moment, her phone rang. Justin.

"Just wanted to tell you I had a good time today," he said.

"You never did get too far away from my door without calling me," she said, touched that he'd remembered. "I had a good time, too."

"See you Tuesday and sleep tight."

With that, Justin was gone, and Chandy leaned back, a huge smile on her face.

TUESDAY CHANDY WENT TO watch Justin play. Because of a last-minute emergency, she arrived late, and his team was already on the field. She took a seat next to Paige, who offered her a bottle of water.

"No beer for baby," Paige said.

"So how did Ahmed take the news?" While they'd sent brief texts, Chandy and Paige hadn't had a chance to catch up.

"Fabulous," Paige gushed and Chandy relaxed. "He was surprised, but thrilled. He thought I didn't want kids because of what we'd talked about when we got married. He never said he'd changed his mind because he didn't want to pressure me. He figured what we had was good, so why ruin it by asking me to do something I didn't want to do. And I didn't want to bring it up, either."

"So all this time both of you had wanted kids and you never talked about it?"

"I know. Weird, huh? Is he not the perfect guy? I got a keeper. You should have seen him when he called his parents and gave them the news. His mother cried.

You know he's an only child. She's been dying for grandchildren."

"I'm so glad everything worked out."

"Better than I'd ever hoped for. It's amazing how sometimes people don't communicate because they think they're doing the right thing. But enough about me. Spill all the details. How was the ball game? How was your date? Don't keep me in suspense."

Chandy told her everything, finishing with, "So this is date number three. It seems sort of surreal. Could this really be it? Could this be our chance?"

Justin gave Chandy a wave as he headed to the dugout when the teams switched places. She waved back.

Paige had watched the exchange with interest. "He obviously likes you and you like him. It could be that simple. You'll just have to see how things go. You're different people, sure, but at the heart of things you're still the same inside. Older, but better. Able to see through the bull."

"I asked him to come to Minnesota, to the lake, for my grandfather's birthday."

"Ooh. That sounds serious."

Chandy nodded. "I know. Maybe I jumped the gun, but he said he'd think about it."

"So have you kissed him yet?"

Chandy blushed. "Yes, but that's all. We're taking things slow on that front."

"No chance of repeating what happened last time."

"None," Chandy said. While she'd told Paige about the miscarriage, she'd kept the part of being unable to conceive again to herself.

"Shame. Now that I've got all these happy hormones I want everyone else to be as happy as me. I do hope you and Justin work out."

Chandy sighed. "I hope so, too. I'm already a bit of a mess. Here I was the one not wanting to move too fast and yet I'm inviting him to come stay with my family after a few dates. I'm such an idiot."

"No, you aren't. He's a very sexy man, and you loved him once. You thought you'd share a life together. Since you already know each other, it's logical not to worry about the little details."

"So do I bring it up again? Do I ask him tonight?"

"Just take things as they come tonight. You want to continue this relationship and if he's not ready to go to Minnesota and see your family then don't push. Trust me, you want to keep the family in the dark as much as possible. Often all they do is meddle and make things worse, especially when things are new and fragile. And despite you two knowing each other, this is new."

Chandy thought of her grandfather and Chase. Her brother already knew some of what was going on. Of course, her grandfather wasn't going to be thrilled. "True. But my family is very close."

"Chandy, you have to do what makes you happy. And if being with Justin is it, then be with him. Follow your heart. You both deserve this chance."

Chandy's phone rang, and she glanced at it. "Speaking of the family." She connected and saw Paige's look of understanding when Chandy said, "Hi, Grandfather."

Leroy's voice boomed in her ear. "Hey, Chandy. Checking in."

Ever since his heart attack five years ago, her grandfather had called Cecile, Chris, Chase and Chandy weekly just to touch base. "So how's everything going?" Leroy asked.

"Great." All around her people cheered at the third out. The teams began to switch sides.

"Where are you?"

"Softball game." Justin was now playing third base.

"Oh. That sounds fun."

"It is. How have you been feeling?" she asked.

"Eighty-five."

"You have a little time left before the big day," Chandy chided.

"Yeah, but it means another party. What is it about years divisible by five? Miranda's got far too many people coming. This was supposed to be a small thing and she's gone nuts. She's carrying twins. She should be taking it easy. But you know how stubborn she is. Two weeks from now this thing will have taken on a life of its own. You'll be here, right?"

"Of course, I'm coming," Chandy said. She took a deep breath and plunged in. "I'm thinking of bringing some friends."

There must have been something in her tone, for Leroy's voice took on an edge. "Who?"

"Justin and Ben."

While she expected she hadn't stunned him—nothing surprised her grandfather—he remained silent for what seemed like a long time. "You couldn't leave it alone, could you?"

There was no accusation in her grandfather's words. He simply stated the facts, as did Chandy. "No. He makes me happy," she told him. "I want this opportunity to try again."

The silence seemed to stretch and then Leroy said one word. "Okay."

She leaned back against the bleacher behind her. Paige was rummaging in the cooler, removing another water bottle. "Okay? That's it?"

"Yeah."

"So you're actually all right with this?"

Leroy sighed. "No, not really. But as you told me over Easter, you're a big girl, Chandy, and you've been on your own for a long time. I need to trust that you know what you're doing even though I have my own reservations."

"Thank you." Chandy felt more confident, and quite relieved. Something wet touched her arm, and she straightened and used her free hand to take the fresh bottle of water Paige offered. "Besides, I don't even know if he's going to agree to come. You intimidate him."

Leroy laughed. "Good. I've got quite a few years on the both of you. With age comes experience. That and arthritis."

"But if he does join me, you have to behave. I like him. You would, too, if you got to know him. He's just like you, actually."

Leroy harrumphed a little and then he told her he loved her and that he'd call when she wasn't busy.

Chandy put the phone down next to her and took a long sip.

"Well, what did your grandfather say?" Paige asked.

"He's not thrilled abut the idea of me being with Justin, but he wants me happy."

"Family approval is important," Paige said with a nod. "It can make things easier or harder."

Chandy contemplated that as they watched the last inning of the game. For once in her adult life, she had the feeling that she was on the right path with a man, that things would somehow work out. And she'd told her grandfather she wanted to bring Justin home.

She had feelings for Justin. This weekend had showed her that. Time had changed each of them, yet it seemed as if they could fall in love again—a new love much stronger than the old.

When she was seventeen she'd sworn she and Justin were destined to be together. Now, at thirty-two, as he jogged off the field toward her at the end of the game, her heart gave a little leap.

Destiny. True love. She was starting to believe in it all over again.

Chapter Eight

Justin walked around Chandy's Jaguar, studying it from every angle. He held a clipboard in his hand, and as he made his visual and tactile survey, he put little check marks in the appropriate boxes.

Watching to Justin's right was Lou, the man who'd done most of the bodywork. He waited while his boss went over everything. When Justin returned a car to its owner, the philosophy was that it went back in even better shape than the day it rolled off the factory assembly line.

The driver's door swung open easily under Justin's touch, unlike when it had first come in. He sniffed, smelling nothing but the aroma distinctive to a new car. He slid his hand over the leather and made certain there weren't any residual spots from cleaning.

He even turned on the headlights, noting where they were focused on the opposite wall. Early in his career, long before he'd had his own place, he'd sent some poor woman out with her headlights aligned to illuminate only the ground ten feet in front of her. She hadn't figured out why she couldn't see well and was always using her high beams until her boyfriend had driven her car, given her a lecture and insisted she take the car back in to get the headlights aligned properly.

Justin had been grateful she hadn't wrecked, and he'd never made that mistake again. It had taken a month before the guys in the shop let him live down his mistake. He ran his fingers over the steering wheel, feeling the seams and making sure they were tight and perfect.

He knew of unscrupulous shops that didn't even replace the airbags but instead filled the cavities with junk. The unsuspecting driver would never know, unless he wrecked again. At McCall's, a minimum of two people did airbag replacement. Justin had personally helped Lou do Chandy's. He didn't want anything to happen to her. He'd been given a second chance, and if things worked out, he wasn't planning on losing her to anything but old age.

He pulled the hood release, and Lou put the hood up as Justin climbed out. Together they went over the engine and the interior of the engine compartment. Even though Chandy's engine hadn't been damaged, the interior walls of the frame had bent and buckled when she'd hit the car in front. Now everything was like new.

"You did good." Justin looked at his sheet. "Just a wheel alignment and a wash and wax."

"She's next in line for the machine and then Zach'll wash, wax and vac her."

"Perfect. So Chandy can get her car tonight?"

Lou thought for a moment. "Anytime after four should be fine."

"Thanks, Lou. She's going to be pleased." The car was perfect.

"Hey, Dad." Ben came through the front door—it was the last day of school and the students had been let out at noon. "What's for lunch?"

"There are some sub sandwiches in the refrigerator."

"Cool." Ben disappeared toward the lounge.

"Hey," Justin called.

Ben came back. "Yeah?"

"After Chandy's car's finished getting an alignment, Zach's going to wash, wax and vac her. Why don't you take over instead?"

Ben's eyes lit up. It meant he'd get to sit inside and drive the car about ten feet to the wash bay. "Can I?"

"Yes. But be aware that I'm going to do the final inspection myself."

"I won't disappoint you," Ben said, and as he headed into the lounge Justin could hear Ben telling Zach that he'd wash the Jag.

With that, Justin settled into his office chair and picked up the phone to call Chandy. While he'd talked to her daily, he hadn't seen her since the softball game, after which they'd all gone to dinner at a local pub. He still hadn't given her an answer about Minnesota.

He really wasn't sure why he was so worried about going. Was it seeing how much money Chandy's family had? Or was it facing everyone after what he'd done? She kept insisting they'd forgiven him, but doubt remained. He hadn't been there when she'd needed him. *But you can be there now*, a voice inside his head reminded him. And there can be other children. Justin had always wanted more than one. He and Chandy had declared in high school that they'd have at least five.

But that was then, and this was now. Each step was important. As with her car, there couldn't be any mistakes.

CHANDY HAD BUTTERFLIES in her stomach as she parked outside of McCall's around six-fifteen that night. First, she was seeing Justin, and when they'd talked this afternoon he'd said he had their night all planned. Second, she was nervous. Justin had told her that was normal. Everyone wondered if the repairs would be noticeable and if the car would handle the same.

Like the first time she'd arrived, she found the place empty as everyone was off at five. Justin had left the door open, and she strolled in, a bell announcing her arrival. He must have been listening for her, because he appeared out of nowhere. "Hi."

"Sorry I'm late. I had two infant emergencies."

He stepped forward and drew her into his arms. "That's okay. Is everyone all right?"

"One has chicken pox and the other was dehydrated, so I sent her over to the pediatric E.R. She needs IV fluids. I'll probably get paged a few times tonight."

When he saw she was finished speaking, he leaned down and kissed her.

The kiss was sweet like a lollipop and Chandy gave herself up to it and let the stress melt away. Then he lifted his lips from hers and stepped back. "Come on, I know you're dying to see your car. I would be." He dropped his arm around her shoulder and led her through the shop.

"I rather liked the kissing, though."

"More later, then."

She tilted her head at him. "Promise?"

"Definitely." He took her to a side yard where her car sat under a carportlike structure. Even though it was still bright and sunny, Justin flipped on the floodlights so that she could see the car clearly. "There she is."

"Wow," Chandy said. She ran her fingers over the hood, feeling the smooth texture of the new paint and clear coat finish. "This is fabulous. I can't tell the difference." She blushed. "Not that I expected to or anything."

Justin grinned. "Sure you did, but that's okay. It's that way for everyone. Well, not the repeat wreckers. I know one lady who has been rear-ended six times. For her getting her car repaired is old hat."

"Hopefully that won't be me," Chandy said. "I'm praying this was my one and only."

"This being your one and only sounds great. I certainly don't want you to have another."

"Me neither."

He pointed. "Open the door. The keys are in it."

She lifted the handle and climbed in. Everything smelled fresh, and she inhaled deeply as she settled into the soft leather. She pressed the buttons, adjusting the seat until she was satisfied. "Much better than what I've been driving."

He leaned closer. "See, no odor. Just like new."

"It's amazing. Thank you."

"Hey, Ben washed it but don't worry, I supervised."

She ran her hand across the dashboard, noting how clean and dust-free it was. "I'm very impressed with the work."

His lips inched into a grin. "Glad you trusted your gut?"

"Glad I listened to all those who told me to bring it here? Why, yes, I am."

He winked. "Well, let's take it for a spin around the block. I have something to show you."

"Do you want to drive?"

"Nope. I've already done that."

She opened her mouth and he put a finger on her lower lip. "Hey, someone had to do the final road test. I'm the owner. I trump everyone."

Once Justin was seated and strapped in, she slowly inched the car out from under the carport and through the gate. She followed Justin's directions. They took the highway westbound, exiting at Pacific. Then he directed her to where one of the main streets had been blocked off for a car festival. "I haven't been to one of these since we went to that one in Leesburg our junior year. That was a good time."

"Which is why we're here," he said.

An impish joy filled her. "Really? This will be fun."

"I told you I had the perfect date night planned. Stop a second."

He climbed out, spoke to someone at the barrier and a few seconds later Chandy was driving through. Classic cars lined the street, and he pointed. "Park there in that open space."

"That's your Vette."

"Yep. McCall's always enters a car in Cruise Night. That's Lou and Steve. They work for me. They'll watch everything so we can walk around."

Chandy backed in next to Justin's Corvette, and a few minutes later she'd met Lou and Steve. They, too, had classic cars. After some chitchat, Justin took her hand and they began to walk down the street. All around, people sat on lawn chairs or stood and talked cars. Justin took her hand and they crossed into the next block where vendors sold food and beverages. His stomach growled, and Chandy laughed. "We need to get you fed."

"Which is where we're going. I made reservations."

They ate in a local Italian restaurant's outside garden, which provided a great view of the Cruise Night activities. In another block a band began to play, and music drifted on the warm air as they ate their food.

"How about a movie tomorrow night?" Justin asked as they began to walk through the streets lined with cars. Night had fallen, yet car headlights and streetlamps chased the darkness away.

"I have my shift at the crisis nursery in the morning, so I could do that."

"How about we do dinner and a movie and then have some you-and-me time?" he asked.

"I'd like that."

"Good." They came back to the cars, finding the crowd had grown. Lou's and Steve's wives had joined the party, as had Ben and some friends from high school.

"We walked over," Ben told Chandy. "Everyone was at our house and we don't live too far away."

"Oh," Chandy said, realizing she hadn't been to Justin's house. She didn't even know where he lived.

But the thought slipped her mind as she got to know his employees and their wives.

"Justin's shop is more like a family," Steve's wife, Cynthia, said as she balanced her wide-awake seven-month-old in her arms. Her two-year-old had fallen asleep in the stroller. The guys had moved off, out of earshot. "If he's bringing you around us he must like you."

"Yeah," Lou's wife, Anne, said.

"We dated in high school," Chandy told them.

"And now you've reconnected. That's so sweet," Cynthia said. She glanced at her cup. "I need a refill."

"I'll get it," Anne said.

"Actually, could you hold Rita for a while? She's heavy." Cynthia passed over her child to Anne.

"So do you like kids?" Anne asked as Cynthia headed over to the coolers.

"Love them. I'm a pediatrician and I volunteer at a crisis nursery," Chandy said, explaining what it was when Anne asked.

"Then you and Justin will work out—he's a great dad. I've got five kids, and you should see him with them. He's fantastic."

"He is a good dad." Chandy kept her smile plastered to her face.

"Well, at least you know when you have kids he'll be there for them. Not like my sister. Hey, Cynthia, did

I tell you what Winnie's husband did? The man is such a loser. He..."

Chandy tuned out the conversation and glanced over at Justin. As if sensing her, he turned, smiled and came over. "Having fun?"

"I am. Everyone is very nice."

"Don't worry. We're not giving her the third degree," Cynthia said.

"Better not be," Justin replied, grinning.

"Nope. We were just telling her how great a dad you are."

"Let's not scare her off," Justin warned.

"We're not," Anne replied. "But she's perfect, Justin. And she works with babies. She can handle the brood of kids you want. How many is it? Four?"

"Five," he replied, laughing as he wrapped his arms around Chandy. She tried to relax, but his words had put a chill in her heart. He wanted five kids? Surely he was joking. But then again, that was what they'd said in high school.

"Things will be winding down soon," Justin told her. "Ben's having a bunch of his friends over. You can come chaperone with me if you like. I know you have to get up early tomorrow."

"Maybe I could stop by for a few minutes," Chandy said, curious about where Justin lived.

The rest of the event flew by, and forty minutes later, she walked in the back door of a small brick cottage just a few blocks over.

When they entered the small family room, they could hear the sounds of music blaring in the basement. *"Rock*

Band," Justin explained. "It's their favorite video game at the moment."

"This is a cute house."

"It's not much, but it's big enough for me and Ben."

"It's all you need," Chandy said.

"Yeah, and the basement's finished, so we spend a lot of time down there."

He led her downstairs, where Ben and three of his friends played the video game. Justin introduced Chandy to everyone and she watched Justin as he made certain all was as it should be.

"What do you want to drink?" he asked her as they returned to the main floor.

She opted for water since she'd be driving home soon. Justin poured her a glass and they sat on the living room couch.

"I'm glad you came tonight."

"It was fun meeting everyone."

He dropped his arm over her shoulder. "They can be rather intimidating. Anne and Cynthia aren't afraid to speak their minds. Their husbands have been with me pretty much since I bought the shop, so we're all pretty close."

"I liked seeing this side of you. Thanks for bringing me tonight. It was nice to feel included."

"I don't want you to ever feel excluded," he said. She didn't answer and he shifted, moving his arm so he could massage the back of her neck. He made small circles with his thumb and fingertips, and she let her head drop forward.

"That feels wonderful," she murmured, and he

continued his magic until he gently turned her face and kissed her. They kissed for a while, stopping when they heard feet pounding up the stairs.

"Hey, Dad?" Ben skidded to a stop in the archway, his eyes missing nothing. "Oh, sorry." He turned his attention back to his dad. "Can I make some of the pizzas in the freezer? We're hungry."

"Sure," Justin said.

"Cool. Thanks. Hey, guys, we can," Ben yelled as he made his way to the kitchen.

Chandy used the distraction to stand. "I should go," she said.

"Really?" Justin glanced at his watch. "I guess it is after ten. And we do have tomorrow night for just us. Alone. With no distractions."

"Perfect," Chandy said. Justin walked her to her car and gave her a goodbye kiss.

The Jag engine purred as she opened it up on the highway. She reflected back on the night with a smile on her face, until she remembered what he'd said about wanting kids.

She drummed her fingers on the steering wheel and took a deep calming breath. Justin was a wonderful father, and she was developing feelings for him. She didn't want to overreact, but maybe she should tell him that she couldn't have children.

No, Chandy decided. If he fell in love with her, really loved her, then he'd understand and they could work through it. But she didn't think they were at that point yet.

She knew he'd feel guilty, and she didn't want to

cause him unnecessary stress. If this new relationship was going to survive, they needed a little time to enjoy each other's company without dwelling on past hurts. And she wanted them to have a fighting chance. She'd tell him she was unable to conceive later. Much later.

SATURDAY STARTED OFF with one of those terrible mornings. Nothing Chandy did could quiet the baby in her arms. She'd tried rocking, burping, pacing, feeding and even swinging, but Sierra just cried. Chandy felt the baby's stomach, but couldn't detect any constipation. Sierra didn't have a fever. Maybe it was just a case of the poor thing badly missing her mom.

"It'll be okay," Chandy consoled. The baby gulped as she geared up for another round of tears. Just then, the nurse came back into the room.

"You look worn down," Lynda said.

"I don't know where this little one's getting the energy."

Lynda reached for the child and Chandy passed her over. "Well, don't blame yourself. When my daughter got like this nothing but a car ride would do. I used to drive around St. Louis for at least two hours a day. Thank goodness gas was cheap then. Here, let's try the swing again. Maybe she's burned herself out enough that it'll work this time. There you go," she told the baby as she strapped her in. But despite the soothing motion, Sierra's continued to cry.

"Go home," Lynda told Chandy. "You look like you could use some sleep yourself."

"It's my seasonal allergies. They kicked in first thing, which rather sucks since I have a date tonight."

Lynda arched an eyebrow. "Same guy?"

"Yep."

"Hmm. Serious."

"I hope so," Chandy said as she prepared to leave.

She drove home, stopping at a fast-food drive-through for a southwestern salad. Justin wasn't picking her up until five, and it was only two. She could catch a few hours of sleep before she had to get ready.

The insistent ringing of her doorbell told Chandy that she'd overslept. She took one look at herself in the dresser mirror and groaned. As she tried to straighten her hair with her fingers, the phone began to ring. She finally reached the door and opened it, grateful that at least she'd worn shorts and a T-shirt during her nap. "Hi. Sorry, I came home and fell asleep."

Justin stepped inside her condo for the first time, a bouquet of roses in his hand. She took them from him, thrilled by his thoughtfulness. Surprise flowers were the best. "Thank you. This is sweet."

"Are you feeling okay?" he asked, leaning down to kiss her.

"Yes. My allergies kicked in so I took a nap. Of course now I'm not ready to go."

He kissed the top of her forehead, his lips lingering for a second. "It's no big deal. There's plenty of time. No hurry. I thought we'd eat around here so we can catch the late show at the Des Peres cinema."

"Then I feel better that I'm not messing up any plans.

Can I get you anything?" Chandy asked as she put the flowers in some water.

He shook his head. "No. I'm good."

"Then make yourself at home and I'll go get changed."

She was ready in less than ten minutes, and was delighted to see that once again Justin had brought the Corvette. He drove them to downtown Kirkwood, where they had dinner at one of the restaurants along Kirkwood Road. It was Chandy's first time eating at this particular restaurant, and she enjoyed the eclectic atmosphere and delicious food. Then they made it to the romantic comedy with enough time to buy some popcorn and drinks.

The movie was a hit, and Chandy and Justin laughed through the entire thing. "That was great," Justin said as they exited the theater. "I hate when movies don't live up to the hype."

"Me, too. And this one wasn't so much of a chick flick that you didn't enjoy it."

"Yeah, some of those movies are pure torture to us guys."

They held hands as they walked to the car. "What shall we do now?" she asked once they'd both climbed into the car. It was after eleven, but she wasn't ready to call it a night just yet.

"I was thinking a stop by Ted Drewes or a late drive or...did you have a suggestion?"

"No, but I could use a kiss." Chandy brought her mouth to his.

"Hey, we need to stop or take this somewhere private."

Justin groaned a few minutes later as he lifted his mouth from hers. The car windows had fogged up.

"Why don't you just take me home?" she suggested, ignoring the voice saying that once again she was moving too fast. But now that they'd reconnected, she wanted the last barrier between them to disappear.

His breath came out ragged. "If that's what you want."

She put her hand on his thigh. "It's exactly what I want. Do you need to be home tonight?"

"No. Ben's staying overnight at a friend's. He won't be home until at least noon."

"Then come home with me and stay awhile."

The drive took only five minutes, but for Chandy, every one of them heightened the anticipation. Her fingers trembled as she unlocked the door to her condo.

He drew her into his arms the moment the door closed behind them. "Don't be nervous."

"I'm not."

"Yes, you are." He kissed her forehead, the tip of her nose and finally her lips. Then he moved his mouth to her neck. "As much as I want you, Chandy, we don't need to do this if you're not ready. The first and only time we made love I moved away the next day and never called you. I understand if you need some time to learn to trust me again."

She placed her hands on his cheeks and moved so she could stare into his eyes. "Are you planning on leaving me anytime soon?"

"No." The determined tightness to his jaw showed that he meant every word.

"Then make love to me. Show me how good we can be together. Let's take that next step. I'm ready if you are."

"Chandy, I'm more than ready. But I've screwed up so badly in the past."

"Then let's put the past behind us."

She lifted her mouth to his, and when he kissed her it was sweet and gentle. His mouth melded to hers, erasing their past and creating a bright future.

Her whole body began to quiver as the sensations produced by his kiss shook her. His lips nipped and teased. Kissing Justin was better than tasting the sweetest nectar. His hands drifted to her hips and he drew her closer to him. Then he swung her up into his arms, carried her to her bedroom, to which Chandy pointed, and used his foot to push the door open. His jaw was set and his step determined. She trembled. He wanted her.

He sat her on the bed and began to undress her. His fingers were gentle as he removed her shirt and then slid one of her pink bra straps down.

In high school their lovemaking had been special but unrefined. Now they made love as adults. He was beautiful. Even at thirty-two he had the body of a god. He worked out, and his chest was firm and hard, his abs a perfect six-pack.

Making love was all about trust and they drove each other to the edge and back as they forged a new future. Finally they lay wrapped in each other's arms, spent.

"That was…" he whispered, at a loss for words.

"Wonderful." Her contentment didn't fade as he

shifted her to a more comfortable position. Her arms and legs felt boneless. Justin's fingertips traced her eyebrows, nose and lips.

"You are so beautiful. Even prettier now than in high school and you were gorgeous then," he said. He touched her lips, and she kissed his finger before he withdrew it. He gave her a kiss. "Tell me what to do next."

"Stay the night," Chandy said.

"You're sure?"

"Yes. You're mine," she told him. He needed to know that. To realize she wasn't letting him go. Not now. Not ever. Not after she'd rediscovered him and caught a glimpse of all they could be together.

"So I am, huh?"

"I call the shots." She was sleepy, and he drew the blanket over them. "You're mine. Get used to it."

"I guess I'll have to because I certainly want to be yours." He drew her closer. "Ben and I will go to Minnesota next weekend."

Even though sleep had almost claimed her, she heard him clearly. "Thank you."

He kissed her forehead, his lips soft. "Sleep, sweetheart. We'll talk in the morning."

"Okay." Chandy drifted off. She was content. Oddly happy—a word she hated to use as she found that happiness often turned into heartbreak. Most definitely satiated. She was sleeping in Justin's arms, and she'd wake up with him in the morning, something she'd never once gotten to do during their relationship in high school and the one prior time they'd made love. She snuggled close. She was finally home.

Chapter Nine

"We're up to seventy-five people coming to the party," Miranda told Chandy during their conversation the following Monday. With Memorial Day weekend looming, and Justin committed to going to the lake, Chandy had called Miranda to make arrangements. The lodge would house Leroy and all four of his grandchildren and their families. Even with five oversize bedrooms, the place would be full, and Chandy didn't want Justin and Ben at a hotel in town twelve miles away.

"Did you already book up the cabins?" she asked her sister-in-law. Aside from the lodge, there were also two additional houses on the property, each about the size of a small double-wide trailer. Both had two bedrooms.

"Walter and his wife are in one, but so far everyone else is staying at the hotel or at the resort on the big island. Why?"

"I need a cabin for Justin McCall and his son. They're coming with me."

"And Justin is the guy you're dating?"

"Yes, Justin and I were high school sweethearts. Ben's his son. And we've rekindled the flame."

Actually, they'd started a wildfire. Justin hadn't left until eleven Sunday morning, and Chandy hadn't gotten much sleep that night. Her pillow had still smelled of Justin and she'd dreamed of him the next night.

"Okay, I can put them in the cabin. You're lucky Leroy's sister isn't coming to stay until the first weekend in June. So I want to hear all about this guy."

Chandy gave her sister-in-law some details. "He sounds wonderful," Miranda said.

"We'll be driving up on Friday. I had to take a shift at the emergency room on Thursday. One of my partner's wives went into labor today—she's a month early."

"Ouch. Hey, I have a better idea. It's at least an eleven-hour drive from where you are and that's on a good day with no road construction. Why don't you let me send the plane? That way you can come up Thursday night and sleep in. I'd offer to fly you Friday, but one of the VPs is doing a surprise inspection of a vendor we're using. We're a bit unhappy about some quality reports. Nothing like showing up before a holiday weekend, when everyone's guard is down, to find out what's really going on. So Thursday night? I'll have the plane on the ground by 6:00 p.m."

"That'll work. I'm off at two, which usually means three, and Justin's working until five. Thanks for offering."

"There are some perks to being a McDaniel, Chandy. You two can fly home Sunday night or Monday morning. Just let me know which you'd prefer," Miranda said.

But as soon as the arrangements were made and she

hung up the phone, Chandy began to worry. Whether she liked it or not, Leroy's birthday weekend was always a show of McDaniel wealth, and they would be flying in on the corporate jet. Heck, the catering alone had cost fifty thousand for Leroy's eightieth party, five years ago. This wasn't a simple backyard barbecue.

"Your one o'clock is already here," Mindy, the nurse, said, poking her head in.

"Is it one?" Chandy asked, surprised. Lunch had flown by.

"No, but you're double booked. For some reason the chicken pox is going around as is a late spring virus. The afternoon is going to be crazy."

Chandy pushed the matter of Justin out of her head. She didn't have time right now to agonize about how they would travel to Minnesota, or what he might think about the travel arrangements. He'd said he was committed to the entire package. Well, here came test number one. Hopefully they'd pass.

"THIS IS SO COOL," BEN SAID. He fidgeted with his seat belt and shifted in the oversize tan leather chair, then flipped open his Nintendo DS. "I can't believe you even have a stewardess."

"Flight attendant," Chandy corrected, reaching for her glass of iced tea. "She's the captain's wife. She travels with him everywhere and can fly as well as he or his copilot can."

"Do you travel like this often?" Ben asked. He'd even read the safety booklet that came with the Bombardier Global Express jet.

"Not really. I usually fly commercial, unless I'm going home." Chandy glanced out the window. They were flying at forty thousand feet, and would be on the ground by eight-thirty at the municipal airport closest to Lone Pine Lake. They should be at the lodge by nine, right in time to greet everyone and chat for a while before bed.

Ben had done most of the talking; Justin was oddly silent. The plane sat eighteen people, and when they'd boarded and he'd realized it would be empty except for the three of them and the crew...well, she knew he thought it was excessive even though he hadn't said a word.

She sighed and drank more tea. She'd told him about the flight on Wednesday. Maybe giving him only twenty-four hours' notice had been a cop-out on her part. But she'd been at the crisis nursery Tuesday and... Oh, who was she kidding? She'd turned into a big chicken.

"Is that a good book?" she asked Justin.

He looked up and shrugged. "So far it's okay."

"What's it about?" He was reading a thriller and she didn't recognize the author.

Justin spent the next few minutes giving her a brief synopsis and as that seemed to break the ice, Chandy relaxed. Her fingers loosened and the tension in her shoulders eased. She leaned back in her chair and opened her own book.

"So who's picking us up?" Ben asked after the pilot announced over the loudspeaker that they'd be landing in twenty minutes.

"Probably one of my brothers."

It was Chase waiting at the airport with Leroy's Lincoln Town Car. They loaded everything into the trunk and spent a minute watching as the jet took off back to Chenille.

"Justin, good to see you," Chase said, reaching out to shake Justin's hand. "And you must be Ben. I'm Chase."

"Yeah. Nice to meet you." Ben shook hands with Chase. The drive to the lake took about twenty minutes, and Chandy sat up front with her brother. Chase kept the conversation humming with questions about life in St. Louis. Darkness had settled over the lake, but the size of the lodge was evident from the lights pouring out every window. "Wow," Ben said.

"You're in this cabin," Chase told them, pulling up alongside a small house. He parked, and Ben and Justin unloaded their stuff.

"I'll walk them up to the lodge after they get settled," Chandy said.

"I'll put your suitcases in your room."

"Thanks."

Chase drove the sixty or so feet to the main house, and Chandy opened the cabin's screen-porch door to let Ben and Justin inside.

"Here is your home until Monday," she said as they went into the vaulted living room.

"Wow," Ben said again, and Chandy smiled. He was, after all, just a fourteen-year-old kid. "Dad, this is bigger than that apartment we had."

"It is," Justin said. The cabin had a great room/kitchen combination with a wood-burning fireplace. There were two bedrooms, and Ben took the smaller one with the lake view. The master-bedroom windows overlooked the meadow where the party would be held.

Chandy pointed to a building near the water. Low-voltage solar lights lined the path down the hill. "The boathouse is filled with games and a pool table and such. It's a teen hangout. My nephews Cory and Clayton like to spend a lot of time there. They're about your age. You'll meet them tonight."

"Sounds cool." Ben threw his suitcase on the bed, clearly ready to go over to the lodge.

Chandy turned to Justin. "Do you want to unpack first?"

"We can do that later. Let's go get this over with."

Chandy took his hand and squeezed it. He was clearly nervous, although he was trying to hide it. This was bound to be tough on him, meeting the whole McDaniel family after fifteen years, and on their turf. She gave him a quick kiss on the cheek. "You'll be fine. Let's go."

As THE WARMTH AND reassurance from Chandy's hand and her kiss traveled through him, Justin forced himself to relax. He could do this. But facing them would be difficult. While they'd accept him because of his and Chandy's current relationship, he knew that deep down they were still wary, worried he'd hurt her again. And as for Chandy's grandfather, Justin didn't expect forgiveness. He'd be lucky if Leroy tolerated him.

As they walked toward the lodge he realized how massive it really was. His home in St. Louis was only slightly larger than the cabin they were staying in, and the McDaniel property had two cabins plus the huge lake house.

He and Ben followed Chandy along a stone path lit by low-voltage solar lights, and then through the professional-grade kitchen with its high-end stainless steel appliances. Everyone was waiting for them in the lodge's great room, which, with its twenty-five-foot vaulted ceiling at one end, seemed more like a hotel lobby than anything. The room screamed old wealth.

The great room contained multiple seating groupings and since there was nothing above the great room, Justin assumed the bedrooms were located in the two-story wing on the far end of the house, opposite the enclosed sun porch. He could see the stairs leading to the second floor, and the open doorway that led to the first.

A fire roared in the stone fireplace—the pinkish stones went floor to ceiling. "Don't touch those," Leroy warned Ben when he went over to look. "We don't have central heat. Those stones can get hot enough to burn your fingers."

Ben turned to face the elderly man who, until that moment, had been reclining in an easy chair. Justin swallowed. Leroy McDaniel at eighty-five was just as intimidating as he had been at seventy.

Chris's boys came up to Ben and introduced themselves. Then everyone was on their feet and saying hello. And even though he'd known Chandy's siblings from before, it was still all very new and awkward. Yet never once did Chandy leave his side, deftly running interference when necessary to keep the conversation light and upbeat.

After about an hour, Leroy announced it was past his bedtime and everyone took the hint to go their separate ways. Ben had long ago disappeared to the boathouse with Cory and Clayton.

"Oh, they know the way," Chris said as he and his wife, Joan, said good-night. "They'll come up to the house when they're ready."

"I'll walk you back," Chandy told Justin.

"I'd like that."

They held hands, the waning moon creating soft light that glowed through the trees and cut a path across the lake. "It's beautiful out here," he said. "You sent me all those pictures but I never imagined it would be like this."

"I know. It's my haven. The lake's beauty was the only thing that made summers away from you bearable."

"I missed you when you were gone."

He'd always felt much more grounded with Chandy around, and the eight weeks she'd spent at Lone Pine every summer had seemed to drag on endlessly.

"At least now you know what the fuss was all about. And you survived tonight."

"Yeah. It wasn't so bad. Piece of cake."

She laughed. "Liar."

"Okay, caught me. This is somewhat hard on me. I'm a bit nervous."

Chandy and Justin sat on the porch swing in the screened porch. "You are a good man. Just remember that."

"I'll try. Although sometimes I think I'll pay for my mistakes forever. I can't forget them."

"You need to let that go. I've forgiven you. And you'll fit in as well as you did fifteen years ago, so don't worry."

"Yes, but back then I was young and naive. I'm pretty wise in the ways of the world now. I'm never going to be rich, Chandy."

"No, but you're everything I've always wanted, and that's what matters. I don't care about money."

"That's because you've always had it," he pointed out.

"Maybe," Chandy said, sighing, "but it's still the way I feel." She put her head on his shoulder and wrapped her arms around his waist. Her embrace felt wonderful. "Let's just run away to somewhere no one knows our names."

"I wish that were possible. We'd have to take Ben, though."

She snuggled closer. "Of course we would."

They sat in silence for a few minutes, just holding each other. "You happy?" he asked.

"Very. And that's what scares me."

He shifted so that he could see her. "What do you mean?"

"It's weird, really. You're nervous about my family, and I'm worried about being happy. It doesn't make sense, I know, but it seems like every time I'm happy, something comes along to ruin it. It's like fate has it in for me."

He wrapped his arms tighter. "Chandy, that's all circumstance. Just bad coincidence."

"Maybe, but it's happened enough times that I believe it. I was so happy with you, and you left. Five years ago, same thing. I received some recognition during my residency and a day later Cecilia called to tell me Grandfather had had a heart attack and they didn't know if he was going to make it."

"Oh, sweetheart." He kissed her forehead. Amazing how life's incidents became scary baggage. "We're quite a pair, aren't we?"

"Yes, and I hope we remain a pair for a long time. Despite our fears and insecurities."

A fierce, protective determination stole over him. "We will make it," he promised.

They heard voices then, as the boys came out of the boathouse. "Here they come," Justin said.

"Probably a good idea on their part. Tomorrow's a big family day."

"Yeah. Ben loves to stay up past midnight, but he doesn't need to be doing that tonight. He should get some rest. What is the plan for tomorrow, anyway?"

"Breakfast in the main house around eight. After that I'm sure Cory and Clayton will want to water-ski. Does Ben ski?"

"He's been once. A friend took us during a fishing trip."

"He'll pick it up quickly. It's like riding a bike. As for fishing, there are no fish in this lake according to my family. No one ever catches anything. It's like the fish laugh at our lures."

"Maybe I can catch something. I'm not too shabby a fisherman."

"Well, around here, that would be one way to get hero status and show us up."

Ben came onto the porch, his tennis shoes thumping on the steps. "Hey," he said as he saw them. "What are you two doing sitting in the dark?"

"It keeps the bugs down. The mosquitoes are the size of birds so be sure you put on repellant tomorrow night." Chandy rose to her feet. "I'll leave you both to get unpacked and see you in the morning."

The porch door creaked behind her, and Justin watched her disappear toward the main house. Ben plopped down in one of the chairs across from his dad. "You should see that boathouse. It rocks. They've got this huge plasma screen and all these games. Cory's only eleven but he's really skilled at playing pool. He beat me three times."

"I'm glad you're getting along with everyone," Justin said.

"Yeah. This is great. Do me a favor and don't screw this up."

Justin frowned. "What do you mean by that?"

Ben's lawn chair had runners, and he rocked back and forth. "Chandy's a great person. I like her. You could do a lot worse. In fact, you have. Remember Vivian? When I was seven? She was a mess."

"Yeah, she was," Justin agreed. She'd been one of the few relationships he'd had, and it hadn't lasted more than six weeks. She'd been possessive and clingy, and she hadn't liked Ben all that much. The feeling had been mutual. Justin had avoided entanglements since.

"I don't know what you saw in her. Anyway, Chandy's different. You're relaxed and happy around her. She seems good for you. And look at this place. She's rich."

"I'm not after her money," Justin snapped, worried that was exactly what all the McDaniel friends and business associates at Saturday's party would think.

"Hey, I know you're not. But having money helps. Besides, it's obvious you like her, so don't blow this, Dad. I like Chandy, too. I could see her as a stepmom. You should marry her."

"Whoa. No one said anything about marriage."

"Why not? It's simple. She likes you and you like her. Fall in love and what do you get? You've always taught me the answer is marriage."

Okay, Ben had him there.

"So don't I get a vote and some input?" Ben continued. "You always say we're a team."

"I do," Justin admitted. "And I take it your vote is for Chandy. I have that under current advisement. But relationships take time and Chandy and I are taking things slow."

"Seems rather dull to me."

"Coming from the man whose relationships have lasted at the most all of a week."

"Hey, I'm only a sophomore."

"Exactly. So you'll have to trust me that I know what I'm doing."

"As if." Ben laughed, and Justin knew his son was

giving him grief. Then Ben sobered. "Just take things slow, Dad, like you always tell me to do," he warned. "Seriously, I like her. She's good for you. She makes you happy. I've never seen you like this. It's nice."

Justin got to his feet and opened the door to the living room. "I'm trying not to ruin anything," he told his son. "Believe me on that."

Chapter Ten

Friday dawned bright, sunny and gorgeous. Chandy slept until nine, and by the time she came down from her bedroom over the kitchen all showered and ready, her entire family was awake and moving about. She'd dialed Justin's cell phone before descending, but no one had answered, so she'd assumed they'd slept in.

However, she found Justin in the great room having a cup of coffee, an empty breakfast plate on the coffee table in front of him. Leroy sat in the mission chair by the front windows reading a news magazine. The older boys had taken the kayaks out and were somewhere paddling around the lake. Miranda's son, Bobby, was with Cecilia, who was in the kitchen making her daughter, Lanie, some toast. Chris, Joan, Chase and Jesse were playing nine holes on the golf course that was barely visible if one looked directly across the lake.

"Good morning, you two," Chandy said, leaning down to give Justin a quick kiss. Then she went to Leroy and kissed her grandfather's cheek. "Sleep well?" she asked them both.

Leroy answered first. "Yep. Like a baby."

"Good," Chandy replied, giving her grandfather a once-over. He looked healthy. She admitted she was a worrier. She knew he wasn't any happier than Justin was with this weekend, but so far her grandfather was trying.

Chandy glanced at the water. "It's pretty calm out there today, so I'm ditching my original sailboat plans and think I'm going to take out the runabout instead. Unless anyone needs it?"

Her sister entered the room, kids in tow. A former dancer, she was still trim and thin, and like all Chandy's siblings, she had blond hair and blue eyes. "No boating for me. I'm going to help Miranda supervise party setups. She's already out in the meadow. I swear that woman never sleeps."

"Do you need me to watch Bobby and Lanie?" Chandy asked.

"No, I've got them. I'm going to head to the store and Lanie's a great shopper. She'll keep Bobby in line. Go enjoy yourself while you can. Tomorrow's going to be hectic."

"Too hectic," Leroy grumbled, but Chandy knew her grandfather would love every minute of the event. He was fond of birthday parties, especially his own, even if he did declare them frivolous nonsense.

"So do you want to see the lake?" Chandy asked Justin.

"You should," Leroy said, looking over the top of the news magazine.

Justin smiled and picked up his plate so he could return it to the kitchen. "Why not."

About 10:00 a.m. she and Justin unhooked the twenty-foot runabout and took to the water. They found the kayakers, and let them know what was going on. The boys decided to ski, and as they were on the south side of the lake past what locals called the big island, they began to paddle toward the lodge. It would take them about forty minutes to return, so Chandy checked her watch and began Justin's tour of the lake.

They cruised close to the big island. "This used to belong to a lumber baron in the 1920s but now it's a resort," she told him.

After she pointed out several other things, and they stopped at the small quick shop around one hundred yards before the place where the lake spilled over a small dam to form the Lone Pine River.

"This is how all the loggers sent the logs to the mills," she said as a store attendant gassed up the boat. Afterward, she drove the boat through a small channel that led to another lake. "This is the best place to ski," she told him. "We'll bring the boys back here. But for right now—" she turned the engine off and let the boat float "—I need you to kiss me."

"I thought you'd never ask," Justin said, glancing around. Tall pine trees surrounded the egg-shaped lake, and if there were any houses, none were visible.

His hands threaded into her hair and he brought his mouth down to hers. Chandy enjoyed every minute of the kiss and the time they spent alone, just the two of them. But all too soon it was time to leave—they were going to be late meeting the boys.

Once back on the main lake, she opened the throttle

and let the boat fly over the water. They found the boys sitting on the dock. "Been here long?" Chandy called.

"Nah. Five minutes. We had a snack," Cory replied. He had a wet suit draped over his arm. Since it had been a cold winter, the lake water wasn't very warm, although the air temperature was perfect.

She tossed Clayton a mooring line, and he secured the boat to the dock. "Are you going to ski?" she asked Justin.

"I'll pass. I'm not a fan of cold water."

She planted her hands on her hips. "Wimp. I'm sure we can find you a wet suit."

He shook his head. "Nope. I'm good with just hanging out and being the spotter."

She winked at him. "Well, I'm skiing." She hopped out of the boat and went into the boathouse to retrieve her wet suit.

They spent the next few hours skiing the same lake Justin and Chandy had been on earlier, until everyone decided they were hungry. Then they headed back to the lodge. By this time, the golfers had returned and the house was full. Ben excused himself to take a shower, and returned twenty minutes later.

"How are things going?" Chase asked Chandy as Cecilia brought out a plate of sandwiches. Everyone was out on the enclosed sun porch for a late lunch, except for Leroy, who'd decided to take a nap.

"Fine," she said. Justin sat at the other end of the table, out of earshot. He was talking to Cecilia's husband, Jesse, about something. "So far Leroy's behaved himself."

Chase's brow creased. "You don't think he will continue to do so?"

"I just got this strange vibe this morning. He says he's comfortable with my dating Justin but it's like he's watching both of us. As if this weekend is a test."

"He is turning eighty-five. Maybe he's feeling his mortality and becoming all sentimental. He only wants you to be happy."

"Please, age has nothing to do with it. He's going to outlive us all. I can easily see him at one hundred-and-ten, still just as stubborn as usual," Chandy said.

"Well, in this case, I think you're just imagining things. He's not going to meddle. He learned that with me."

Chandy began to believe Chase might be right as the day went on without incident. After lunch, Justin disappeared with the guys to play billiards in the boathouse, leaving the women to head outside and make sure the party preparations were on schedule.

Out in the meadow the grass had been cut, and large crews had arrived to install huge open-air tents. Tables and chairs appeared, and the party company set up a small stage for the band. Five years ago Chandy hadn't been as involved, as she'd been doing her residency. Now she stood next to a very pregnant Miranda, who managed to both balance her son and direct everything that needed to be done.

"You can tell why Leroy hired her to be an executive," Joan remarked. Chris's wife had come out to see what was happening.

"I can also see why Chase fell in love with her,"

Chandy said. "Who else could boss him around so well?"

"She's definitely his perfect match," Cecilia agreed, looking up from her review of the band's set list. "Which brings us to you, Chandy. We are all curious about this thing with you and Justin. Just how serious is it? Will we be hearing wedding bells in your future?"

Chandy's heart gave a small, excited jolt. She'd dreamed that very thing last night. "We've just started dating again. There's so much history between us that we have to work through."

"Yeah, but at the same time you've known him for years. You can bypass the stupid stuff," Cecilia pointed out.

"Maybe, but then again we're different people. And I haven't told him I can't have kids."

"Oh," Cecilia said. She seemed temporarily at a loss. "Do you think that matters?"

Chandy told them about the conversations during Cruise Night.

"Wow," Cecilia said. She patted Chandy's shoulder. "I feel for you."

"The question is, do you love him?" Joan asked.

"Yes."

"Then everything will work out," Joan said.

"My life doesn't work that way," Chandy said.

"Then tell him the truth. If you love him, and he loves you, children shouldn't be an issue. They may symbolize love, but children aren't what causes love to deepen." As a preacher's wife, Joan had a lot of experience helping couples and families with their relationships, and her words were always insightful.

"Your life could also be less stressful. Kids can strain a marriage." Miranda approached. She'd overheard the conversation. "Not that that's what's happening in mine, but I'm just saying. It happens in plenty. And Justin has Ben."

"He's always wanted a big family," Chandy revealed.

"Aren't you more important than that?" Cecilia asked.

"I hope so," Chandy said, glancing over her shoulder toward the lodge. "I sure hope so."

DESPITE HIS EARLIER reservations, Justin found himself enjoying the weekend. Chris and Chase seemed to accept him, which was a good thing, because if he ever did marry Chandy, they'd be brothers-in-law. He got along well with Jesse.

The weather for Saturday's party was sunny and perfect. Even though the dinner festivities didn't start until four, guests began to arrive as early as noon. This gave Justin a chance to watch Chandy interact with family friends and neighbors.

This was her home, her element. She knew everyone, or if not, they knew her and talked about how much she'd grown. It touched his heart that she included him and made sure he wasn't left out.

As he held her close later that night during a slow dance, he had to admit that he'd been wrong. His fears had been baseless. While he'd gotten a few speculative looks, most people had taken him at face value.

Even Walter Peters, Leroy's best friend and a McDaniel board member, had been welcoming. Justin and Leroy had spent about twenty minutes talking classic cars, with Walter even offering to buy Justin's Corvette sight unseen. Justin had told him no, and Walter had laughed and said he'd had to try.

"Enjoying yourself?" Chandy asked as they stepped together to the music.

"I am," Justin admitted. "I love holding you like this."

"Glad you came?" she pressed. She slid her arms around his neck.

"So far," he said. "Although it's been crazy. Nonstop. I'm glad we got to sneak off for a little while earlier."

Since Ben had been with Cory and Clayton, Justin and Chandy had been able to get away for a while during the party. Unnoticed, they'd hidden out in the cabin for an hour and made love.

She nestled her head into his shoulder and he liked it. "Tomorrow will be much calmer. We'll go to brunch at the country club. After that let's try to get some more alone time like we did a few hours ago."

"I'd like that," he said. While his relationship with Chandy wasn't about sex, she completed him. Touching her and holding her was a way to express how he felt. Which was?

That he loved her. He'd never stopped. He'd closed a part of his heart when he'd moved to Chicago, but now that they'd reconnected, the floodgates had opened. He loved her—both the Chandy of the past and the woman she'd become.

They danced the night away, until the party began to wind down around eleven. By midnight only the catering staff remained, and they were cleaning up. The next morning the party company would come and haul all the tents and tables away, leaving the meadow in its natural state until next year.

Justin walked Chandy back to the lodge, where he kissed her good-night. He opened his mouth to tell her how he felt, but then Chris's sons had arrived, interrupting the moment, and Chandy had slipped inside to play aunt.

Ben was in the cabin when Justin entered.

"So did you have fun, Dad?" Ben asked.

"Yeah, I did. I've had a great time. The McDaniels are good people."

Ben hesitated. "Can we come back?"

"We haven't left yet. And it's up to Chandy."

However, the idea didn't seem as scary anymore. He loved her. He repeated the words in his head, finding them much to his liking. He loved her. He'd tell her tomorrow.

Everyone slept in, and it was after a delicious and boisterous brunch that Leroy pulled Justin aside. "I'd like to talk to you later," he said. "Alone."

"Okay," Justin agreed, although the thought of speaking with Leroy one-on-one ended his jovial mood and instead filled him with anxiety. But he steeled himself. He was no longer a child, and it was time to meet Leroy as a man. He loved Chandy and wanted a future with her. He would do whatever was necessary.

"What did my grandfather say?" Chandy asked. Everyone was in the great room so they couldn't have a very private conversation.

"He wants to talk later."

"Oh. I guess I don't need to see the movie."

"No, you go. I'll be fine."

"Sure?"

He could see her worry. "Yes."

"Okay." She bit her lower lip, and Justin reached forward to touch her cheek.

"It'll be okay."

Later, before Leroy's nap, Justin settled himself into one chair in the great room and Leroy took another. Justin clasped his hands in his lap, and then realized that made him look nervous and put both his hands on his knees.

Leroy was known for being direct, and he didn't waste any time but got right to the point. His blue eyes were razor-sharp as he locked gazes with Justin. "So what are your intentions toward my granddaughter?"

For this question he was well prepared. "I love her."

Leroy studied Justin with the precision of a defense attorney. "You said that fifteen years ago."

Justin tried not to squirm. If he and Chandy were going to have a future, he needed to win over Leroy. He had to make him understand that he'd never hurt Chandy again.

"Chandy and I have discussed what happened," he said. "We've made our peace with it."

"You know she lost your baby."

"I do and I feel terrible about that. She shouldn't have gone through that alone. You should have let her call me."

"And what would you have done?"

"Does it matter? I deserved to know," Justin said.

Leroy shook his head. "I did what I thought was best."

Justin shifted uncomfortably. "Chandy and I have had to really clear the air, and we deserve this second chance. It hasn't been easy for either of us to get to this place, but I love her and I want a future with her."

They sat in silence, the ceiling fan high above making a low whirring noise.

"You were never my first choice," Leroy said finally. "I'll admit to being somewhat snobby at times, but I've worked hard to get where I am."

"As have I."

Leroy acknowledged that with a slight nod. "Yes, you've done quite well for yourself. I did some research."

Justin clasped his hands together. "I don't want her money."

"No, that you never did," Leroy acknowledged, and Justin could tell Leroy believed him.

"Anyway, when she met you I figured it was a passing phase. You know, a crush. But I met my Heidi in high school and when I saw Heidi, she was the only one for me. Chandy was like that with you."

"And me with her, sir."

Leroy tapped his fingers on the chair. "Maybe. But I don't think you truly understand how powerful the love you two shared in high school was."

"No, sir, I do. I went crazy without her. I made dumb mistakes. I imploded."

"Yeah. You threw it all away. If you really understood how important your love was, how could you have done that? She waited for your phone calls. Stood by the mailbox so certain that today would be the day she received a letter. Daily I watched her hope die."

Pain lanced Justin's heart. "I was selfish. I went from star athlete to someone who wouldn't go to college. I self-destructed. I couldn't bear to call and tell Chandy how far I'd fallen. I figured she'd be better off not knowing since there was no way to fix the situation. That was a mistake. We've talked about it extensively, and while we've moved forward, you are right. I was an ass. I can't ever make up for what I did up to her. But I plan to spend the rest of my life trying. I love her. I always have. She's my world."

"How can you be so certain that this time it will last?"

"Because I'm no longer seventeen. I'm thirty-two. I know what I want—I want to be with Chandy, to build the family we always dreamed of."

"Do you know why Chandy spends so much time at the crisis nursery?"

"She loves children."

"I want you to ask her the real reason."

Justin stared at Leroy. "I don't understand. Please

don't play games with me, sir. Tell me what you're getting at."

"You took something from her, something more than her heart. You took her hope. She told you she lost the baby, but did she tell you the rest?"

Justin dug his fingers into the hem of his shorts. "No. You've totally lost me."

"Please ask Chandy to tell you the rest. If you really love her, you need to know. There can be no secrets if this is going to work between you."

Justin stood, confused. "Is that what you want?"

"Yes and no. I realized something yesterday. I'm old. I want her to be happy, and I need to be certain that you will bring joy to her life."

"You don't think I will."

"I believe you can. She's been happy lately. She's falling in love with you all over again. Not that she ever really stopped, I suppose. Are you up for that responsibility now?"

"I believe I am."

"I hope you're right."

Justin left the lodge, heading down to the dock. He grabbed one of the runabouts and took the boat out onto the water. Fittingly, clouds were rolling in and the surface was choppy. He headed to the lower lake, which was sheltered by heavy trees, then turned the engine off, letting the boat bob as he ran over the events that had brought him to this point.

Chandy had been pregnant with his child. She'd been seventeen and alone. He could picture her surprise. Her fears. Her joy. Somehow, although he hadn't been there, it was as if he could see everything. It was as if they were linked. He felt her pain, her despair as the days grew and he didn't contact her. Her ultimate sorrow when she lost the baby. He saw her picking herself up. Going to college. Becoming a doctor. Working with children, to whom she gave everything.

In contrast, he'd been so outright selfish. He'd been so focused on what he'd lost that he'd never once considered her feelings, or the stress he'd caused her. If he truly had… He stopped. He couldn't undo anything. He'd royally screwed up.

And Leroy had suggested there was more. Something he had to ask her.

She was sitting on the dock when he returned, her arms wrapped around her knees and the breeze toying with her hair. She was waiting for him, a worried look on her face. As he pulled up alongside, she stood and reached for the rope so she could moor the runabout. "My grandfather left me a note saying you took the boat out."

"Did he tell you anything else?"

She shook her head. "He's already in bed for a late nap. Did you have a fight? Did he upset you?"

He raked a hand through his windblown hair. "No. No fight. He just told me I needed to ask you something."

"What?"

"He said, 'She told you she lost the baby, but did she tell you the rest?'"

Her face paled. "Oh."

He quickly climbed out of the runabout and went to her side. "What is it?"

"Nothing."

"Chandy. We need to be honest with each other. You have to tell me." He tried to wrap her in his arms but she stepped away.

"Justin, let's not ruin things. That's what's going to happen."

"You don't know that."

"Yes, I do. The guilt over what happened already weighs on you. I don't want to cause you more pain."

"Whatever it is, it can't be that bad. We'll get through it. Your grandfather already told me what an idiot I was for throwing our love away and not being there for you. I've spent the past hour berating myself."

"Then let's not add to it."

"Tell me."

She dropped her gaze to her feet, and then slowly looked back up at to meet his eyes. "I can't have any children."

"What? You were pregnant."

Her voice dropped and he had to listen closely to hear her. "When I lost the baby I had a bacterial infection. The doctor said I could no longer have children. As a doctor I understand it. But as a female, I don't." She was close to tears.

He grasped the implications. "I did this to you."

"See, I knew that's what you'd say. No one did it. It was just fate. That damn fate that never lets me be happy."

Justin looked at the woman he loved. Leroy was right. She deserved someone who wouldn't cause her pain.

How could she even look at him after what he'd done? He'd ruined her ability to create life.

"If you hadn't been pregnant. If I hadn't left…"

"If, if, if." She was becoming more distressed. "There's no point in asking 'what if?' But see what I mean? Everything was so perfect. We were in love. I was happy. And then the rug got pulled out from under me. You left. I lost the baby. And I lost the dream of being a mother, something I had always wanted."

"Oh, Chandy."

"No, don't you pity me. You can love me, but you cannot pity me. Just what else did he tell you? Did he try to buy you off? Did he pay you to go away?"

Justin shook his head. "No, of course not. I'd never take money and you know it. He told me how much pain I'd caused you, but he also said he thinks we can get through this. But how can you forgive me? I ruined your ability to have children. You love children and you're so good with them. I took that away from you. It's my fault." He never could have imagined this. He'd given her the worst life sentence imaginable.

She held on to one word. "Fate."

He touched her arm. "Don't give me that. Don't lie and say you don't blame me, because I can see from your expression that deep down you do. Don't tell me you're okay with what I did. I replaced you and a woman I didn't love gave me the son you'll never have. How can you look at us? Look at me?"

"Because I love you."

She jerked away and the tears broke free as fifteen years of rage exploded. "I always have. But it wasn't enough. Why did you leave me? Why? Ben should be my son. His mother doesn't even want him. I wanted my baby. I loved it from the very first moment I knew I was pregnant."

She drummed her fists on Justin's chest. He let her beat him, knowing he deserved the blows. "Do you know how much therapy I've had? Why did this happen to me? Do I have to lose everything I love? My parents? You? My baby?"

She screamed her anger into the wind, years of guilt finally finding an outlet. He knew she'd been carrying this tragedy for far too long.

"It's okay." Justin held her close, letting her vent. Her fists didn't really hurt, and he deserved whatever she dished out. "Let it out. That's right. Let go, Chandy. Hate me if it helps. I ruined your life. You need to stop hating yourself. It's my fault. I'll carry the burden from here. You need to let it go."

Her lips quivered and her hands fell to her side. "I waited for you. I needed you to be there."

"I know you did. I'm so sorry I wasn't there." He steadied himself. He might not ever be okay in the grand karma of the world again, but whatever living hell he endured from this moment forward, he had earned. Chandy had suffered for fifteen years—now it was his turn.

She nodded. "You didn't love me enough. You didn't believe in us."

Justin shook his head as the truth he'd denied for so long became clear. "No, I didn't."

She looked at him sadly. "I can't give you the children you want."

"I don't need children."

"You don't mean that. I heard you say you want at least five."

"I used to think I wanted a big family, so that I wouldn't feel so alone. But now I realize that what's important is being with you. And Ben, of course."

She held up a hand. "I'm sorry, my head is pounding. I think I need to lie down, to be alone for a while."

He approached and she waved him off. "No, I can take care of myself."

She'd been doing just that for a long time, Justin knew. He nodded. "I know you can. That's why I'm going to give you all the time and space you need. I'm going to take Ben and head back to St. Louis in the morning as scheduled."

"That might be wise. Maybe we were moving too fast. Maybe we can't recapture what was broken. I just don't know anymore."

He'd never told her he loved her, and knew the words were meaningless now. When it had really counted, he hadn't loved her enough. "You deserve to be happy, Chandy. I want to be with you, but I can't keep hurting you."

He leaned over to briefly kiss her forehead. She closed her eyes at the touch. "We can talk later, on your terms. You need space to think."

"Yes, I always do." He watched her leave the dock, her arms wrapped around herself. He glanced up the hill toward the house, but no one was at the picture windows. Chandy headed around to the back where she could escape to her bedroom over the kitchen unseen.

Justin went to the cabin. Ben was playing his Nintendo, Cory and Clayton having gone somewhere with their parents.

"Hey, we need to get ready to head home in the morning," Justin told him.

Ben set the game aside, his eyebrows knitting together. "Are you okay?"

Justin shook his head. "No, I'm not."

"Did something happen between you and Chandy?"

"It's a very long story. You're going to have to trust me on this one and just not ask me to explain right now. But, yes, Chandy and I have some things to work through."

Ben frowned. "That makes no sense."

Outside, lightning cracked and thunder boomed as a late storm arrived. The barometer had dropped, but the low pressure wasn't to blame for the oppressive weight on Justin's shoulders. "Ben, sometimes things don't work out. We're staying over here tonight and not going to the lodge."

"Okay." Ben got to his feet and headed to his room.

It didn't surprise Justin that Chandy wasn't with Chase when he picked them up and drove them to the airport the next morning as scheduled. Chase said little, and Justin even less. The flight home took an hour, and Ben and Justin were retrieving their car from a lot at the Spirit of St. Louis airport less than two hours after leaving Lone Pine. Justin watched as the jet took off, back into the sky.

"Coming Dad?" Ben asked, ready to get home to all his friends. After all, it was summer vacation. His life was still wide-open and full of fun possibilities.

"Yeah," Justin said, finally turning back to his son. "I'm coming."

Chapter Eleven

"Chandy?" Chase called. She heard him open the door below and next his footsteps as he came upstairs to her hideaway over the kitchen. Chase's head poked around the corner. "Are you decent?"

Chandy pulled her covers up to her chin. "Go away."

"I just thought you'd want to know that they're gone," Chase said.

Justin and Ben hadn't come over to the lodge, staying in their cabin instead the previous night. Once she'd finally gone downstairs, she'd remained only five minutes before retreating. Obviously Ben and Justin had flown home as scheduled. "Thanks for letting me know."

Her brother entered and took in her appearance. She knew she looked like a wreck. "I figured something was up when you didn't show and he didn't mention your absence. Want to talk about it?"

"No."

His brow creased. "Maybe you should. Grandfather's awake. He wants to see you when you come down."

"I'm not talking to him, either," Chandy snapped.

Her heart lay shattered and, like Humpty Dumpty, all the king's men couldn't put it back together again. "Just tell me when the plane's back from taking Cecilia, Lanie and Jesse to New York so I can fly home sometime today."

"Chandy…" Chase was clearly at a loss for what to say to his distraught sister.

She sat up and glared at him. "Take the fees for the extra flight out of my trust fund."

He threw his hands in the air, frustrated. "You know it's not that. But from what I saw, you and Justin were happy. Good together. Whatever happened, I'm sure you can fix this."

She'd cried most of the night. "No, it's too complicated. I don't think we can work things out. And for the record, I'm the one calling it off."

Chase's voice cut through her misery. "I thought once that things in my life were beyond repair. I was wrong."

She eyed her brother suspiciously. "With who, Miranda?"

He nodded. "Yes. You know we had a rocky start. She was all set to become the McDaniel CEO after Grandfather sent me on sabbatical. When I came back and took over, I displaced her. But work didn't make me happy. Being with her did. Somehow, despite everything, including my royal screwups, I convinced her to take a chance on me. I couldn't be happier."

"I'm not like you. Being with Justin hurts. I can't have children, and even though he says he's okay with that, I know he wants children. How can I be with him, knowing he's giving up something he values? Eventually he would come to resent me."

Chase winced. "I'm sorry."

"It's like I've lost him all over again but this time it's on my terms. Sometimes when you relight a fire all that happens is that you get burned. You'd never understand."

"Maybe not. But I do know one thing. It's about what you want, about what makes you happy. I could have stuck my head in the sand and let Miranda get away, but I realized that life without her was much worse than any fight we'd ever had. If you want him, you'd best go after him."

"No. It's for the best that I sent him away. I told him I needed time, but I just don't think I can risk my heart on him again. All that pain just came flooding back, and it's more than I can bear."

Chase sighed and bent down to wrap his arms around her. "Okay. If you need to talk you know where I am."

He straightened and walked toward the door, turning to face her before he left. "I also came up here to tell you that Chris and Joan are leaving within the hour to drive back home. Will you come say goodbye?"

"I'll be there," she replied.

"Good." Chase gave her a sympathetic smile before he headed back downstairs, leaving Chandy to her misery. She got up, went to the mirror, and said the daily affirmations she hadn't needed to say since her first date with Justin. But saying them felt hollow, as if, in her heart, she knew that she was fooling herself.

A few hours later, besides Chandy, only Chase,

Miranda, their son and Leroy remained at the lodge. Miranda and Chase were staying until tomorrow, but they were in their bedroom suite at the moment, putting Bobby down for a nap. Chandy wouldn't leave until the pilot called and said he was within an hour of the airport.

"I'm sorry," her grandfather said when they were finally alone in the great room.

She fingered the cotton throw she'd covered herself with from the waist down. The rain last night had ushered in chilly temperatures. The day was wet and gray and the lake sat empty, whitecaps forming and frothing. How many times lately had she been hearing the words *I'm sorry?* "Let's not talk about it."

"I didn't mean for you to send him away."

She looked over then. Her grandfather seemed even smaller today. Chase had built a fire in the fireplace, but Leroy still looked cold, even with a blanket over his legs. "Are you feeling okay?"

"I'm tired," he told Chandy, but smiled reassuringly. "I'm not going anywhere, so don't worry about me. I have to make sure you're going to be okay first. Besides, Heidi says it's not time yet. I hear her talking to me sometimes."

Chandy's fingers tensed. Hopefully her grandfather wasn't getting senile. "And what does she say?"

"That she loves you and wants you to be happy. That I should stop meddling so much. I try to do the right thing. I thought I was."

There was no point in berating her grandfather. "It's okay. You meant well. I still love you."

"But do you love Justin?"

Chandy sighed. "I thought I did. Maybe I was just trying to reach for something that doesn't exist."

Leroy seemed sad. "Happiness exists. You can't let what happened when you were a teenager color your world any longer. Take the brass ring and grab it."

"But what if there isn't a ring? What if I'm not supposed to have true love?"

"Never think that. You will have love. You might have to work at it, but you can't give up trying."

"Easier said than done."

Leroy's gaze locked on to hers. "I might have complicated things for you, but I also exposed the truth that you've been avoiding. Ask yourself, what will make you feel better? When you figure out what that is, you'll find peace and happiness."

"I've been trying."

"Try harder. Dig deeper. It's your life, Chandy. What is it you really want?"

Chase exited the upper hallway and came down the stairs into the great room at that moment. "Chandy, the plane will be on the ground in a half hour. If we leave now we'll be there when they land. Are you ready?"

She stood. "Yeah, I am."

THE FLIGHT BACK HOME was uneventful, and Chandy read her book.

It wasn't until the following weekend at the crisis nursery that she really thought about what her grandfather had said.

Earlier in the week Paige had called Chandy's avoidance of problems the ostrich syndrome. Chandy simply buried her head in the sand. She pretended that she didn't miss Justin's text messages or phone calls, and that she enjoyed the silence.

She'd sent him away. He wouldn't initiate contact.

"Here you go," Lynda said, handing Chandy a two-month-old baby. "This is Will."

"Hi, Will," Chandy said, taking the baby into her arms. He had pale skin and a tuft of dark black hair. "He's a tiny thing."

"He was a preemie. He's had a rough start," Lynda said, handing Chandy a bottle.

"Well, let's get you some food," Chandy said. She tilted the bottle and slipped the nipple into the baby's mouth. Will began to suck hungrily. "There you go. Poor little guy. Such a sweetheart."

Sweetheart. A term of endearment Justin had always used. She shifted, making the glider begin to move. Will ate three ounces and Chandy put him over her shoulder and began to rub his back gently. He emitted a huge burp, and Chandy moved him into the curve of her arm. As the glider moved back and forth, the motion put him to sleep.

She didn't move him, even after her arm became numb. She rocked, holding someone else's baby. Her grandfather had asked her what she really wanted. She wanted this. She wanted a baby. A child growing within her. A life that she would bring forth and love. She wanted what she couldn't have.

Oh, sure, she knew she could always adopt. She'd considered that. She had the financial resources to adopt at home or abroad. Chandy had enough love in her heart for dozens of children. But the process took years.

One thing was for certain—she'd wallowed long enough.

If she wanted happiness, she would have to create it herself. And it was about damn time she did.

DETERMINING TO DO SOMETHING and actually doing it are two different things, and Chandy found herself not as far along on her plan as she'd like, a fact her friend Paige noticed and pointed out two weeks later.

"You know, you really look terrible," Paige said as she exited a patient's room in the pediatric E.R. Her white coat snapped about her legs and hid her baby bump.

"Thanks for the compliment. I love you, too." Chandy read the chart in front of her. "Don't you have a patient to go stitch up or something?"

"Just finished. So what's wrong, other than the obvious heartbreak?"

Chandy took a deep breath, trying to release some of the tension she'd been carrying since Memorial Day weekend. "I don't know. My allergies are on overdrive and I'm just exhausted. Gotta love stress."

"Have you seen anyone?"

Chandy pursed her lips and tilted her head. "Please. I'm a doctor. A little sleep and antihistamine and I'll be good as new. Heck, maybe I'll even get a deep tissue massage. I know how to take care of myself."

Paige's dubious expression indicated how well she believed that. "If you really wanted to take care of yourself, you'd call Justin, kiss and make up. It's obviously you miss him."

"I told you the story. It's over. I'm moving on with my life. If nothing else, this experience finally got me out of my fifteen-year funk."

"Well, I'm not sure you're in a better place."

Chandy put the chart down. "Excuse me?"

Paige folded her arms across her chest. "Come on, you have a minute. This place isn't that crowded, and Bryan's on duty."

The fifty-something doctor exited a room, and Paige took the chart from Chandy's hands. "Bryan, Chandy's under the weather. Can you take this one for her so she can have a quick break?"

She thrust the chart at Bryan and he grappled with it. "Yeah, I guess that's fine."

"Great. Thanks. Jules, did you hear that? I'm borrowing Chandy. If you need us we'll be in the doctors' lounge for the next ten minutes."

The head nurse nodded her assent as Paige cupped Chandy's elbow and guided her toward the staff lounge. Once inside, Paige shut the door behind them.

"You look like crap," she told Chandy again, having the audacity to grab Chandy's white coat so she could study her better.

Chandy tugged her coat back and took a step away. "I told you. Allergies. They're just lasting longer than usual for some reason. The mold count is abnormally high. The weather guy said so on the news last night."

Paige gave her another once-over and rubbed her chin. "It's more than that. You've lost weight and you didn't really have any to lose. This stress is not good for you, Chandy. You can't keep this up."

Chandy had noticed that her clothes had been looser around the waist. She really hadn't been eating enough, either, but then cooking wasn't a high priority. She'd just felt so emotionally drained.

"I haven't been myself since I got back from Minnesota," Chandy admitted. "I think I'm just stressed out over what happened with Justin."

"You're falling apart. Maybe you need to take a vacation or something. Go to the beach. Or a spa."

"I'll be fine. I got over him once, and I can do it again. At least he knows everything now. While I don't feel better, I don't feel as guilty, either. That's making progress, right?"

Paige crossed her arms. "You're really worrying me with how you're talking. You've lost the love of your life twice. Stresses like this take a toll, and your body is obviously manifesting your stress into physical symptoms."

"I told you, I'm fine," Chandy insisted.

"As one of your close friends, I refuse to lie to you, or to let you lie to yourself. You aren't fine. If these symptoms don't go away, I want you to see someone. If nothing else, you can talk to Ahmed. If it's something emotional causing these physical symptoms, he can help. That's his specialty. I don't want you getting any more run-down, okay? Justin looks bad enough. But you're far worse."

Chandy's ears perked up. "You've seen him?"

Paige winced. "I wasn't going to tell you. You're

already under enough pressure... His team played Ahmed's last week. But before you ask, I didn't talk to him. Ahmed did, but he's a guy so he's excused. I glared at Justin for you the whole game."

Chandy could picture Paige sitting on the stands doing just that. "Thanks, I think."

Paige patted her arm. "See? I'm your friend, and since I can tell that you aren't taking decent care of yourself, someone has to do it. You won't be any good for those babies if you don't figure out what's wrong with you."

Rocking the babies was what had been keeping Chandy going. She'd been volunteering extra hours at the crisis nursery as she thought about what to do next. She wanted to make a difference. Sort of like how the founders of the crisis nursery had seen a need and filled it. But she was still trying to figure out the details.

The door to the lounge opened and Jules popped her head in. "I don't mean to bother you, but we've got incoming. A semi plowed into a school bus full of kids. We're getting a bunch of the victims and the ambulances are on their way. Paige, can you stay? More than likely we're going to need a plastic surgeon."

"I can stay." She gazed at Chandy. "We'll talk more later."

Chandy nodded as adrenaline pushed away the doldrums. The kids came first. "Let's get to work."

FRIDAY NIGHT. COLD BEER. Juicy burgers and hot fries. Cardinals baseball on the TV. Poker. All the elements for a perfect evening. But even though he was hanging with the guys because Ben was at a friend's house, Justin wasn't having a good time. All he had to do was look at the green seats behind home plate, whenever someone came up to bat, to be reminded how much he missed Chandy. It had been four weeks now.

"Will you stop thinking about her? I'm finally out of my house for a night with the boys and you're bringing me down, man," Lou said.

"I don't know what the big deal is. You used to be the one who could attract all the ladies. Not that you ever wanted any of them, which of course helped us," Dan said.

He worked construction. He and Justin had become friends when he'd done the expansion on Justin's auto body shop four years ago. Dan had just divorced his third wife six months ago, so Justin didn't necessarily consider him an expert on relationships.

Steve, their usual fourth for poker, was on vacation in Gulf Shores, Alabama, so Lou's brother Larry was filling in. He tossed three blue chips into the center. "Calling, you guys," he said.

Normally they played at Steve's, but tonight they were all at Justin's. Dan tossed his chips onto the pile. Justin looked at his hand, decided that two kings were not going to cut it and folded. His stack of chips had dwindled dramatically.

"Not your night," Dan commented.

"Doesn't seem like it," Justin said. "Nor yours."

"Maybe you should make it up to whoever she is," Larry said, as he won the hand and swept up the pile of chips.

"This is more than a box of chocolates can cure," Lou said. As a few more hands went on, the guys filled Larry in on Justin's love life, ignoring Justin's protests that his life wasn't an interesting topic.

"Yeah," Larry agreed at the end of the story. "He needs to do something big."

"Gee, thanks. I don't think there's anything I can do. She told me she needed space and she hasn't contacted me in four weeks," Justin said. "It's obvious we're through." He tossed some red chips into the center of the table to get the hand started. "Ante up."

"Women never want space," Lou said, dealing out the cards. "They want you to admit you're wrong."

"I have apologized. You don't know Chandy. She's different."

"Send her some flowers so she's thinking about you," Dan said, indicating he wanted another card. "Flowers never hurt."

"Says the man who has a standing account at the florist," Lou said.

"Well, I need one. I don't think I'm the type to be married. I keep trying it on but it doesn't work. I like women too much to want just one. Besides, flowers make them happy, and happy women like to have sex."

"Maybe I should get Martha flowers the next time we fight," Larry said.

"It works," Dan encouraged with a nod. "She'll be putty in your hands."

They all stopped for a minute to watch a double play on television. The Cardinals retired the Cincinnati

Reds to end the top of the inning and a pizza delivery commercial came on.

"Try the flowers," Lou told Justin as they continued play. "What can it hurt?"

"Nothing," Dan agreed.

"But she doesn't want anything to do with me." Justin contemplated the idea.

"Do you want her back?" Larry asked.

"Yes. I love her."

"So tell her. Say it with a card. Women like cards—makes you look romantic. If she doesn't want to talk, she'll just ignore you like my wife does me."

"Do any of you have happy marriages?" Justin asked.

Lou raised his hand. "Me. You know I love Anne and I'm man enough to admit it. Besides, she's hot and she's a great cook."

All the guys nodded. Lou was right on both counts. Justin played a few more hands, his mood lightening considerably. He'd needed this night with the guys. He lost another hand and threw his cards down. "Damn it."

"You suck," Dan remarked.

"Maybe you should call her," Lou suggested.

Justin sighed. "It's going to take a miracle to get us back together and I don't have that kind of magic. Heck, I'm already down twenty dollars."

"And I'm up. Thanks for inviting me," Larry said with a grin. "Those were some good burgers you grilled, too."

Dan gave a cheer as a Cardinals player scored. For

a second Justin wondered if Chandy was at the game. Then he grabbed the cards and started to shuffle. For once he needed to do the right thing. She'd asked for space. It was her happiness that mattered, not his. As much as he loved her, he had to give her what she wanted.

DESPITE ALL HER REASSURANCES to Paige, by the last few days of June, Chandy didn't feel any better. She'd even taken a rare sick day the previous week to try and get extra sleep, but that hadn't helped. She'd felt so bad that she'd swapped her Cardinals tickets over the weekend for dates later in the season. She just hadn't felt like going to the game.

She unlocked the door to her condo after returning from a full day at the practice. Already she was doing physicals for the upcoming school year as parents tried to get those in early. She was tired and it was only Monday. Unfortunately, she had a full schedule the rest of the week.

Maybe she did need a real vacation. She hadn't taken one in the past two years. She'd been so busy working and building her patient list that she'd forgotten to take a break.

She could always head back to Minnesota for the upcoming July Fourth weekend. Or she could simply take some time to do local travel. There was Kansas City and the Harry S. Truman Library. Or perhaps she could drive to Springfield, Illinois, and visit all the Abraham Lincoln sites.

Mr. Wu began to weave through her legs and a wave

of nausea hit her. She felt her glands, which didn't seem enlarged at all. Maybe tonight she'd just lie down and sleep some more. She resolved to call her doctor in the morning.

DR. ELIZABETH JORDAN was one of those no-nonsense internists who really knew her stuff. Chandy had known Dr. Jordan since she'd attended one of the doctor's lectures as a first-year medical student.

As a professional courtesy, Dr. Jordan worked Chandy into the schedule as her last appointment on Tuesday. Once she got Chandy on the exam table, she poked, prodded and listened. And she asked dozens of questions.

She reached for a lab order form. "I'm sending you off to get your blood levels checked. I'm asking for a full diagnostic. I'm checking for mono, iron levels, potassium levels, red and white blood counts, platelets, celiac disease, diabetes and the works. If it can be tested, I'm requesting it."

"I'm sure it's all going to come back fine," Chandy told her. "I think I must have picked up a virus from one of my patients or something."

"Well, before we look for some strange mystery virus, let's see what the tests say. If everything is normal we'll take the next step," Dr. Jordan said.

Dr. Jordan belonged to a huge group of doctors, and the medical practice had a lab onsite. Before Chandy left the office, the technician had drawn three vials of her blood.

She arrived home about a half hour later, after

stopping at the supermarket and picking up an Italian salad for dinner. Yet once she got home she simply couldn't eat it. Knowing the lettuce would look even less appetizing the next day, she tossed the package in the trash can and heated up some chicken noodle soup instead.

The following morning, Chandy struggled to get out of bed. She had a pounding headache, and didn't even want to contemplate eating breakfast. Still, she managed to get to work and put on a good front. Dr. Jordan's office called her around one on her cell phone. "We have your test results. Are you able to see Dr. Jordan at three?" the nurse asked.

"Sure," Chandy told her, and rearranged her schedule.

A few minutes after three Dr. Jordan entered the exam room where Chandy sat waiting. She closed the door behind her. "I know what's wrong with you. First of all, you're anemic."

Immediate relief overtook Chandy. Anemia. No wonder she was tired and woozy. Her iron levels were low. "That's easy to fix. I'll just have to take iron supplements for a while," Chandy said.

Dr. Jordan smiled. "And prenatal vitamins. That's the second thing. Given your first miscarriage, you need to go for an ultrasound immediately. That's why I've called you in. I'm sending you down the hall to Dr. Anderson. He's expecting you."

Chandy was lucky she was sitting, or her knees would have given out. Chills ran up and down her spine.

"There's no way I'm pregnant. I had an infection. I'm sterile."

Dr. Jordan glanced at the chart again. "Then there's a star in the sky because, Chandy, you're pregnant. The blood work is positive."

Chandy somehow found her voice. "You ran a pregnancy test?"

"I told you I was requesting the works. It's part of the package."

"But there's no way I'm pregnant."

"Chandy, we're doctors. We both know that sometimes cancer goes into remission for no other reason than someone said a lot of prayers. Maybe the doctors got your diagnosis wrong fifteen years ago. Have you practiced safe sex?"

"We didn't use anything. I never have. There was no point if the guy was clean." Not that she'd had that many lovers anyway.

"When was the last time you had sex?" Dr. Jordan asked.

"Saturday night, Memorial Day weekend. A few times before that."

"That could be the right timeline. Your anemia may have made you more sensitive to the hormonal changes than normal."

"But those few times in the past?"

"Maybe you've been playing Russian roulette for years and this time the chamber had a bullet in it. The ultrasound will be final proof. Plus, I want a complete picture of what's going on. Because, if you are pregnant, and believe me, the blood work says you are, you're going to be considered high risk because of your previous miscarriage and infection."

"Oh, my God." Chandy's entire body shook. She was pregnant. She was having a baby.

"Chandy?"

She glanced up, tears streaming down her face so hard she could hardly see.

"You do want this baby, don't you?" Dr. Jordan asked.

Chandy put her left hand on her stomach. "More than anything."

Chapter Twelve

The ultrasound later that afternoon confirmed that Chandy was pregnant. She wasn't very far along, but there, in her womb, was a baby with a heartbeat.

She left Dr. Anderson's office with prenatal vitamins, iron supplements and orders to get at least nine hours of sleep a night. He planned to monitor her once a week throughout the entire pregnancy because of her previous complications.

She arrived for her scheduled volunteer work at the crisis nursery with the black-and-white ultrasound picture tucked inside her purse. She performed her volunteer duties in a daze. If all went well, she'd rock her own baby near the end of next February. She got home at eight and called Chase right away. Miranda picked up.

"Chandy, hey, what's up?"

Chandy took a deep breath. "Hi, Miranda, I want to come up there this weekend for the Fourth of July festivities."

"Where, you mean Lone Pine?"

"Yes. Grandfather's still there, right?"

"Of course. He's staying until Labor Day, like he does every summer. We're driving up tomorrow and staying for the weekend."

"I have to work tomorrow, but I'll be off on Monday. Can you send the plane tomorrow evening so I can hang out with you all?"

"Sure. Are you okay? Chase told me you've been sick."

Tears began to fall as Chandy heard the worry in her sister-in-law's voice. "I'm fine. It's nothing. I just don't want to be alone on this holiday."

"I understand. Can you be at the airport by six? Is that too early?"

"I'll be there."

THE FOURTH OF JULY HOLIDAY weekend was one of Justin's favorites. The softball league had its final tournament starting on this beautiful Friday evening, and the only sour note was that since his team had a rematch against Ahmed's, Paige Walter was once again giving him the evil eye as she had the entire game last time the two teams had met.

He wished she'd stop. He had enough guilt on his shoulders without her adding to it. At a break between plays, while Ahmed was in the bathroom, Justin went over to tell her just that.

"Paige."

Her tone was cool and icy. "Justin. Did you need something?"

He nodded. "Actually, yes. You can quit giving me the go-to-hell look. I'm already there."

Paige seemed surprised by his directness, but she rallied quickly. "As you should be. Chandy's my best friend and you hurt her."

"That was never my intention and for the record she broke up with me. I love her and I always will, but I want her to be happy."

Paige shook her head, even more disgusted. "Why do men always say that?"

"Because it's the truth? She asked for space. She called things off. I have to respect her wishes."

Paige's nose wrinkled. "Why? If you love her, you should fight for her. Women like that."

Justin stared at Paige. She lifted her sunglasses and pushed them atop her head. "Look, I probably shouldn't tell you this but I'm worried about her. She's not doing well. She's been sick. The stress of what happened is really wearing her down."

Justin's chest tightened. "I didn't know."

"Of course not. You're giving her space. Do you really believe she wants that? She loves you. Fight for her—sweep her off her feet. As much as I hate to admit it, you're good for her."

Paige reached out and thumped his ball cap. "So go see her, tell her you love her and try not to screw it up this time. I'd hate to have to glare at you all next season, but I will if necessary."

Justin straightened his shoulders and took a deep breath. "I will make this right. I want her to be happy."

Paige smiled. "Well, you're probably the only one who can take away the stress she's carrying. Now get out there and let my husband's team win so he doesn't come home crabby."

Justin laughed and jogged out onto the field where the players gathered. The match was much more even than their previous competition, but Justin's team still won by two runs.

He was grabbing his gear so he could go home when Paige approached. "Sorry, I tried," he told her. "Hope Ahmed's not too grouchy."

"He'll be fine. Listen, I got a text from Chandy during the game. She's headed to Lone Pine Lake. I talked to her Tuesday morning and she wasn't planning a trip. Chandy isn't that spontaneous."

His gut twisted. "Something's wrong."

Paige was genuinely concerned. "But what? She said she was going to see a doctor Tuesday afternoon but I haven't talked to her since. We've been playing phone tag all week. I just tried to call her but her phone's off."

Raw determination consumed Justin. "I'll find out what's going on and let you know."

"You really do love her, don't you?"

He nodded. "Very much."

"Then you better tell her that."

CHANDY ARRIVED AT LONE PINE around 7:30 p.m., and Chase picked her up at the airport. His first words were, "You've lost weight." His second were, "You look like hell."

"Thanks. I love you, too."

"So what's wrong?"

"I'll tell you about it when we get to the lodge. I only want to go through this once."

He risked a glance at her. "You're not dying, are you?"

"No."

"Cancer?"

"No."

"Okay, I guess I can wait."

"Thanks. Just trust me on this. It's good news."

Leroy and Miranda were waiting for her when Chandy arrived. She grabbed a glass of water while Chase whisked her luggage to her bedroom. Then she followed him into the great room. Miranda rose to her feet and gave Chandy a huge hug. Leroy remained seated, and Chandy gave him a hug and a peck on the cheek.

"So what's going on?" her grandfather said.

Chandy sat in the chair across from him. She dug into her purse, pulled out the ultrasound picture and passed it over.

"What's this?" Leroy asked. "Can't see it very well without my glasses."

Miranda, who'd been leaning over, said, "That's a sonogram."

"Why does she have one of yours?" Chase asked, confused.

"That's not mine," she said, studying it. "There's only one baby. Mine showed two."

"That's my ultrasound. I'm having a baby," Chandy said, and for several seconds no one spoke or moved.

"What?" Leroy said.

Chandy took a deep breath. "I'm pregnant."

Leroy stared at her in disbelief. "That's not possible."

Her voice was shaky and full of tears. "That's what I thought, but I am definitely pregnant."

"The doctors all said…"

Tears brimmed in her eyes and poured over, tracking down her cheeks. "They must have been wrong. I didn't believe it myself. My doctor figured it out—it's why I've been so run-down. Well, I had anemia for a while first. But I'm going to have a baby."

Miranda had her hand over her mouth, clearly unsure what to do. Chase leaned over to his wife and put his hand on her shoulder. "This is a good thing," he whispered in her ear. "A very good thing."

Leroy leaned his head back for a moment, and then he straightened, smiled and wiped the tears from his eyes. "That boy certainly likes to knock you up, doesn't he?"

"I've never used birth control since the miscarriage. Not that there were very many times or people but…"

"I so did not need to know about your sex life," Chase interrupted. Miranda punched him. "Ow."

"Congratulations," Miranda said, her own tears starting. "You are happy, aren't you?"

Chandy nodded. "Very. My obstetrician is going to monitor me weekly but he doesn't foresee any problems."

"That's wonderful," Miranda said.

"This is such a blessing." Leroy got to his feet and bent down to give Chandy a big hug. For a while everyone just talked about miracles, and then finally Leroy asked, "So are you going to tell him?"

Some of Chandy's elation evaporated. "Yes. But you're my family—I wanted you to know first. Whether Justin is involved or not, I'm having this baby."

"Of course you are," Leroy said. He'd regained his composure. Surprises never threw him for long. "You're a bright, successful young woman. You have plenty of money. Nothing wrong with being a single mother these days."

"So what about Justin?" Chase asked.

"I'll tell him and we'll take it from there. I want him involved from the beginning this time. I don't know if we'll try to rebuild our relationship, but he deserves to know the truth."

"Can you forgive him?" her grandfather asked.

"For what? Giving me another baby?"

"No, for the past." Leroy gave her a small smile. "You're getting a second chance. Both of you need to forgive yourselves and forgive each other. It's time to focus on the future."

"I need to call him," Chandy said. "Although I don't want him to learn I'm pregnant over the phone."

"Go see him when you get back," Chase suggested.

She nodded and pressed her hand to her stomach as she'd been doing constantly. "I will."

THE FIRST SET OF FLOWERS, a dozen red roses, arrived at Lone Pine Lodge at 9:00 a.m. Saturday morning. They were addressed to Chandy, but had no sender.

The delivery boy shrugged when asked who sent them, accepted his tip and went on his way.

The next delivery came around 11:00 a.m., this time a basket filled with an assortment of flowers including daisies and carnations. The third delivery arrived at 1:30 p.m. and was another bouquet of roses, this time white long stems with red tips.

"Place is starting to look like a darn flower shop," Leroy complained after another delivery arrived at three-fifteen. Once again no card accompanied the delivery, which like the others was addressed to Chandy McDaniel.

"Whoever's sending them must have staggered them," Miranda said.

"It has to be Justin. Who else could it be? I've been trying to get ahold of him all day but his phone is off. Why would he do this?" Chandy asked.

She'd even called Paige, who had told her all about her conversation with Justin, and that she'd told him Chandy's current whereabouts. Paige had no idea where Justin might be, but agreed that the flowers had to be from him. She'd also squealed with delight when Chandy had told her the real reason she was so run-down.

It was a little after 4:00 p.m. when the open windows carried in the sound of crunching gravel. "Someone's here," Chase said. He walked into the sun porch and whistled. "Nice car."

Chandy had followed him. In the driveway sat a 1969 Corvette. Justin stepped out, carrying a huge bouquet of roses.

Chase chuckled. "More flowers. Leroy's going to love this."

"He'll deal," Chandy said, happiness starting to bubble inside her. She poked Chase in the side. "Go let him in."

"Me? He can see you clearly. You can do it yourself."

Justin could see her. He'd stopped walking and was gazing through the open windows. "Hi, Chandy," he called.

"Hi." She went and opened the porch door and Justin came up the steps and inside. "I assume you're my anonymous admirer?"

"I am." He passed over the bouquet of roses. This time they were red with white tips and they were gorgeous. "I wanted you to know I was thinking about you and one dozen didn't seem like enough."

"You sent me flowers and drove up all this way to tell me that?"

"Yep. I heard you were here. Thought I'd drop by." A rustle told them Chase had left the sun porch, and that they were alone.

She tried to keep a straight face, but couldn't help smiling. "Paige told you where I was."

He nodded. "Among other things. We had an interesting talk."

"She told me about that when I called her after the first batch of flowers arrived."

"Well, then you know why I'm here. I love you and I'm here to fight for us. I don't want us to be apart ever again."

"So you drove eleven hours to tell me you love me."

"I didn't say it enough before, and I want you to know that your love—if you can love me again—is enough. I'm also here to grovel if necessary because I want to spend my entire life loving you. I know you can't have kids, but you and I are what matter. We shouldn't dwell on what we lost in the past. We should go forward and celebrate what we have."

"You've really thought about this."

"It was a long drive. I also realized I had to forgive myself in order to be there for you. All my experiences brought me to this moment, and while I may not be perfect, I've grown a lot over the years. I know that I can be the man you need me to be now."

She responded by kissing him. She and Justin loved each other, and this time, it would be enough.

"I've been trying to call you all day," she said when they came up for air.

"I didn't want to have to take my hands off the wheel. I drove the Corvette because it's fast. I was worried about you—Paige said you've been unwell."

Chandy's heart pounded. "I was. But the doctors discovered the cause and I'm going to be fine. Better than fine."

"So it's nothing serious?"

She could see how concerned he was. "No. Actually the opposite. I'm a doctor and I needed blood work to tell me what was wrong. I should have realized, or suspected, but I never believed it could happen to me."

She grabbed both of his hands and looked him in the eye. "I'm pregnant."

He was so stunned he sputtered. "But...but... How is this possible?"

"The doctors fifteen years ago must have been wrong. It's been known to happen." She winked. "I have a scan in the other room. I'm due in late February."

"We're having a baby."

"Yes." Tears clouded her eyes again, but she wasn't the only one crying. "It's like a miracle. The doctor said that everything should be fine."

"It is a miracle. You. Me. Baby. Ben. And we're going to be together." Her big strong man could cry, and she loved him for it. "We're getting a second chance."

"We are, and you do realize you're going to have to do the right thing by me. I'm old-fashioned that way," she said.

He gathered her into his arms, pulling her close. "I'm never leaving you again. Chandy McDaniel, I don't have a ring, and I'm not on my knees, but I love you. I have since the very first moment I saw you in eighth grade. Will you marry me like we always planned?"

She reached up to kiss him. "I thought you'd never ask."

LEROY SHUFFLED THROUGH the kitchen on his way outside. He knew exactly what he wanted to do.

"Hey, where do you think you're going?" Chase asked, catching up. They'd all been watching Chandy and Justin, until the kissing started. Then they'd beaten a hasty retreat.

Chase's grandfather grinned, hand on the door to the outside. "You said he was carrying flowers. Five bucks says the keys to that car are in the ignition. This being the country and all."

Chase appeared to be taken back. "You know what the doctor said. No motor vehicles. You're not driving Justin's Corvette."

A wicked gleam came into Leroy's eyes. "Nope. You are."

Chase laughed. "Well, when you put it that way, let's take that baby for a spin..."

JUSTIN BROKE OFF THE KISS when he heard the familiar roar of a 1969 Corvette engine starting. He turned around in time to see Chase wave and Leroy give him two thumbs-up as the car went racing down the driveway, gravel flying. "They just stole my baby."

Chandy turned his face back toward hers and reached up to kiss him again. She knew he wasn't all that upset. "What can I say? They left you alone with this one. Welcome to the family."

Epilogue

Chandy McDaniel McCall was late. Here it was March fourth and the little girl she was carrying had so far refused to make her appearance.

"Maybe the doctor underestimated your due date," Cecilia consoled her. Everyone was at Justin and Chandy's new house in Kirkwood, the one they'd bought in October. Ben had been ecstatic over the news that his dad was marrying Chandy, and was even more excited about being a big brother. Even the cat liked the changes—Mr. Wu could often be found sleeping on Ben's bed.

"Your C-section is scheduled for two days from now so you know there's an end in sight," Cecilia continued.

"I'm as big as a house," Chandy complained.

"There's no way you're as big as I was," Miranda said. She'd delivered two healthy twins in November.

"You've only gained thirty pounds. I gained fifty," Paige reminded Chandy. Paige had delivered a boy in January. They'd named him Ahmed Joseph, Joey for short.

"Still, this bed rest is killing me," Chandy complained. "First I was anemic, and then she shot my blood pressure sky-high. This kid is going to be trouble."

"She'll be an angel," Cecilia predicted, giving Chandy a pat on the hand as a contraction wracked her body. "All babies are. And I think that's finally a real contraction."

Chandy turned wide-eyed. "And I think my water just broke."

Cecilia grinned and helped Chandy out of bed. "Even better. Let's get your husband. I do believe it's time."

Alexandra Heidi McCall made her appearance ten hours later, at 12:15 a.m., March 5. The entire McDaniel family, Ben, and Justin's mother and brother were present at the hospital for the blessed event. Not one person there had dry eyes, because everyone understood the significance of the date. Sixteen years earlier a baby was lost. Sixteen years later, a new miracle life took its place.

That afternoon, around 1:00 p.m., the family finally gave Chandy, Justin and Lexi some much-needed space after a long night and morning. Justin watched as his beautiful wife nursed their daughter.

"Do you think she waited on purpose?" Chandy asked him.

"I don't know," Justin said, reaching for Chandy's free hand. "But it certainly gives the first week of March a new meaning."

"A year ago I never would have thought this was possible," Chandy said. "I love you so very much."

"And I love you."

He leaned over to kiss her on the lips. "You look very happy."

"I am." Chandy smiled then, her face radiating love. She was happy, and she'd found the happiness that lasted. It wouldn't fade or go away. She and Justin had found each other after a long absence and rebuilt their lives. They had been blessed with that most precious love that would last a lifetime.

And the proof of that love sighed and slept in Chandy's arms, her daddy right nearby as he always would be.

* * * * *

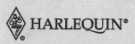

COMING NEXT MONTH

Available October 12, 2010

#1325 THE TRIPLETS' FIRST THANKSGIVING
Babies & Bachelors USA
Cathy Gillen Thacker

#1326 ELLY: COWGIRL BRIDE
The Codys: The First Family of Rodeo
Trish Milburn

#1327 THE RELUCTANT WRANGLER
Roxann Delaney

#1328 FAMILY MATTERS
Barbara White Daille

REQUEST YOUR FREE BOOKS!
2 FREE NOVELS PLUS 2 FREE GIFTS!

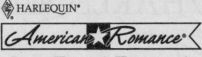

HARLEQUIN®

American Romance®

Love, Home & Happiness!

YES! Please send me 2 FREE Harlequin® American Romance® novels and my 2 FREE gifts (gifts are worth about $10). After receiving them, if I don't wish to receive any more books, I can return the shipping statement marked "cancel." If I don't cancel, I will receive 4 brand-new novels every month and be billed just $4.24 per book in the U.S. or $4.99 per book in Canada. That's a saving of at least 15% off the cover price! It's quite a bargain! Shipping and handling is just 50¢ per book.* I understand that accepting the 2 free books and gifts places me under no obligation to buy anything. I can always return a shipment and cancel at any time. Even if I never buy another book from Harlequin, the two free books and gifts are mine to keep forever.

154/354 HDN E5LG

Name _____ (PLEASE PRINT)

Address _____ Apt. #

City _____ State/Prov. _____ Zip/Postal Code

Signature (if under 18, a parent or guardian must sign)

Mail to the Harlequin Reader Service:
IN U.S.A.: P.O. Box 1867, Buffalo, NY 14240-1867
IN CANADA: P.O. Box 609, Fort Erie, Ontario L2A 5X3

Not valid for current subscribers to Harlequin® American Romance® books.

Want to try two free books from another line?
Call 1-800-873-8635 or visit www.morefreebooks.com.

* Terms and prices subject to change without notice. Prices do not include applicable taxes. N.Y. residents add applicable sales tax. Canadian residents will be charged applicable provincial taxes and GST. Offer not valid in Quebec. This offer is limited to one order per household. All orders subject to approval. Credit or debit balances in a customer's account(s) may be offset by any other outstanding balance owed by or to the customer. Please allow 4 to 6 weeks for delivery. Offer available while quantities last.

Your Privacy: Harlequin is committed to protecting your privacy. Our Privacy Policy is available online at www.eHarlequin.com or upon request from the Reader Service. From time to time we make our lists of customers available to reputable third parties who may have a product or service of interest to you. If you would prefer we not share your name and address, please check here. ☐

Help us get it right—We strive for accurate, respectful and relevant communications. To clarify or modify your communication preferences, visit us at www.ReaderService.com/consumerschoice.

HAR10R

HARLEQUIN®

A Romance

FOR EVERY MOOD™

Spotlight on

Inspirational

Wholesome romances
that touch the heart and soul.

See the next page
to enjoy a sneak peek from
the Love Inspired® inspirational series.

*See below for a sneak peek at
our inspirational line, Love Inspired®.
Introducing HIS HOLIDAY BRIDE
by bestselling author Jillian Hart*

Autumn Granger gave her horse rein to slide toward the town's new sheriff.

"Hey, there." The man in a brand-new Stetson, black T-shirt, jeans and riding boots held up a hand in greeting. He stepped away from his four-wheel drive with "Sheriff" in black on the doors and waded through the grasses. "I'm new around here."

"I'm Autumn Granger."

"Nice to meet you, Miss Granger. I'm Ford Sherman, from Chicago." He knuckled back his hat, revealing the most handsome face she'd ever seen. Big blue eyes contrasted with his sun-tanned complexion.

"I'm guessing you haven't seen much open land. Out here, you've got to keep an eye on cows or they're going to tear your vehicle apart."

"What?" He whipped around. Sure enough, mammoth black-and-white creatures had started to gnaw on his four-wheel drive. They clustered like a mob, mouths and tongues and teeth bent on destruction. One cow tried to pry the wiper off the windshield, another chewed on the side mirror. Several leaned through the open window, licking the seats.

"Move along, little dogie." He didn't know the first thing about cattle.

The entire herd swiveled their heads to study him curiously. Not a single hoof shifted. The animals soon returned to chewing, licking, digging through his possessions.

Autumn laughed, a warm and wonderful sound. "Thanks,

I needed that." She then pulled a bag from behind her saddle and waved it at the cows. "Look what I have, guys. Cookies."

Cows swung in her direction, and dozens of liquid brown eyes brightened with cookie hopes. As she circled the car, the cattle bounded after her. The earth shook with the force of their powerful hooves.

"Next time, you're on your own, city boy." She tipped her hat. The cowgirl stayed on his mind, the sweetest thing he had ever seen.

*Will Ford be able to stick it out in the country
to find out more about Autumn?
Find out in HIS HOLIDAY BRIDE
by bestselling author Jillian Hart,
available in October 2010
only from Love Inspired®.*

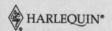